THE LEGACY SERIES

SERIES TITLES

Your Place in This World
Jake La Botz

I Felt My Life with Both My Hands
Jessica Treadway

Hands
Pardeep Toor

Lafferty, Looking for Love
Dennis McFadden

This Is How We Speak
Rebecca Reynolds

All That It Seems
Jim Landwehr

All Gone Now
Michael Tasker

Apple & Palm
Patricia Henley

Bodies in Bags
Jamey Gallagher

A Green Glow on the Horizon
Dawn Burns

How We Do Things Here
Matt Cashion

Neon Steel
Jennifer Maritza McCauley

Release of Information
Kali White VanBaale

The Divide
Evan Morgan Williams

Yes, No, I Don't Know
Kathryn Gahl

The Price of Their Toys
John Loonam

The Caged Man
Calvin Mills

A Day Doesn't Go By When I Don't Have Regrets
J. Malcolm Garcia

These Are My People
Steve Fox

We Should Be Somewhere by Now
Stephen Tuttle

Burner and Other Stories
Katrina Denza

The Plan of Chicago
Barry Pearce

Trust Issues
K.P. Davis

Adult Children
Laurence Klavan

Guardians & Saints
Diane Josefowicz

Western Terminus: Stories and A Novella
Michael Keefe

Like Human
Janet Goldberg

The Hopefuls
Elizabeth Oness

Never Stop Exiting
Michael Hopkins

Broken Heart Syndrome
Anne Colwell

The Mexican Messiah: A Novella & Stories
Jay Kauffmann

Close to a Flame
Colleen Alles

American Animism
Jamey Gallagher

Keeping What's Best Left Kept Secret
David Ricchiute

Soaked
Toby LeBlanc

The Path of Totality
Marie Zhuikov

Shocker in Gloomtown
Dan Libman

The Continental Divide
Bob Johnson

The Three Devils and Other Stories
William Luvaas

The Correct Response
Manfred Gabriel

Welcome Back to the World: A Novella & Stories
Rob Davidson

Greyhound Cowboy and Other Stories
Ken Post

Close Call
Kim Suhr

The Waterman
Gary Schanbacher

Signs of the Imminent Apocalypse and Other Stories
Heidi Bell

What We Might Become
Sara Reish Desmond

The Silver State Stories
Michael Darcher

An Instinct for Movement
Michael Mattes

The Machine We Trust
Tim Conrad

Gridlock
Brett Biebel

Salt Folk
Ryan Habermeyer

The Commission of Inquiry
Patrick Nevins

Maximum Speed
Kevin Clouther

Reach Her in This Light
Jane Curtis

The Spirit in My Shoes
John Michael Cummings

The Effects of Urban Renewal on Mid-Century America and Other Crime Stories
Jeff Esterholm

What Makes You Think You're Supposed to Feel Better
Jody Hobbs Hesler

Fugitive Daydreams
Leah McCormack

Hoist House: A Novella & Stories
Jenny Robertson

Finding the Bones: Stories & A Novella
Nikki Kallioy

Self-Defense
Corey Mertes

Where Are Your People From?
James B. De Monte

Sometimes Creek
Steve Fox

The Plagues
Joe Baumann

The Clayfields
Elise Gregory

Kind of Blue
Christopher Chambers

Evangelina Everyday
Dawn Burns

Township
Jamie Lyn Smith

Responsible Adults
Patricia Ann McNair

Great Escapes from Detroit
Joseph O'Malley

Nothing to Lose
Kim Suhr

The Appointed Hour
Susanne Davis

PRAISE FOR
Your Place in This World

Jake La Botz writes like the bastard spawn of Denis Johnson, Hubert Selby, and Flannery O'Connor. His prose is as haunting and deep as the dark, beautiful, twisted heart of life itself. *Your Place in This World* is the kind of book you don't just read, you stop people in the street and tell them they have to read. It's that kind of good. I loved these stories.

—JERRY STAHL
author of *Permanent Midnight*

La Botz's dialogue is fierce and kinetic, revealing the back-alley wounds of survival that bloom beneath our skin. He ferries us through Chicago streets with the precision of someone who's lived every note, every scar, every song. This collection vividly depicts the pulse of finding ourselves through the grit and endless noise. Get a copy of this brilliant beauty, pronto. Sublime!

—MEG TUITE
author of *Planked by the Abyss*

Jake La Botz's *Your Place in This World* has an emotional depth and street-smart verisimilitude reminiscent of works from writers like Saul Bellow, a gestalt of characters on the outs but still moving, still searching for meaning in a changing world. This book announces the arrival of a gifted new voice—a writer whose lyrical sensibility is eerily reminiscent of Kerouac and who understands how the convergence of place, personality, and circumstance can shape lives and destinies. An absolute feat of a debut.

—DANIEL PEÑA
author of *Bang: A Novel*

Jake La Botz's *Your Place in This World* is a vibrant and delightful ride through a ramshackle realm occupied by addicts and winos, truants and grifters, cheaters, dreamers, chumps, and bluesmen. This world's denizens are hungry, urgent, funny, flawed, broken, resilient, and deeply human. In other words, they are us. Their dreams, schemes, and desires will resonate with readers who have at times felt marginalized or misunderstood. In this world there might not be redemption or even luck—just the reality of your existence, the prospect of a new day, and the sublime comedy of life as you shuffle through the liminal spaces along the fringes of society, maybe, just maybe finding your place.

—LOUIS GREENSTEIN
author of *The Song of Life*

In a collection that is understated and emotionally stunning, Jake La Botz explores the ache and beauty of the dispossessed. He evokes the grit of Chicago, and landscapes beyond, as his characters search for a way to belong. The tonal variations in these stories–from gritty to humorous to magically realistic—are united by the leitmotif of flawed fathering, which gives a heartfelt and resonant undercurrent to this kaleidoscopic collection. In the titular novella, the protagonist, like Joyce's Stephen Dedalus, seeks a father figure to guide him, and finds a mentor in a bluesman who is both blessed and cursed by his ability to give voice to those who have passed on. La Botz's searing details and ear for the longings of our imperfect lives create a collection of stories that shimmer against the dark world they illuminate.

—ELIZABETH ONESS
author of *The Hopefuls*

YOUR PLACE IN THIS WORLD

a novella & stories

Jake La Botz

CORNERSTONE PRESS
UNIVERSITY OF WISCONSIN-STEVENS POINT

Cornerstone Press, Stevens Point, Wisconsin 54481
Copyright © 2026 Jake La Botz
www.uwsp.edu/cornerstone

Printed in the United States of America.

Library of Congress Control Number: 2026931133
ISBN: 978-1-968148-39-3

All rights reserved.

This is a work of fiction. Names, characters, businesses, places, events, and incidents are either the products of the author's imagination or used in a fictitious manner. Any resemblance to actual persons, living or dead, or actual events is purely coincidental.

Cornerstone Press titles are produced in courses and internships offered by the Department of English at the University of Wisconsin–Stevens Point.

DIRECTOR & PUBLISHER
Dr. Ross K. Tangedal

EXECUTIVE EDITORS
Jeff Snowbarger, Freesia McKee

EDITORIAL DIRECTOR
Brett Hill

SENIOR EDITORS
Paige Biever, Lhea Owens

PRESS STAFF
Samantha Bjork, Sophie McPherson, Karlie Harpold, Lillian Kulbeck, Natalie Daute, Bud Halverson, Jazmyne Johnson, Grady Roesken, Aja Wooley, Andrew Bryant

To my daughters, Raven and Lottie

CONTENTS

Your Place in This World   1

March 15th   105

Sponsors   110

Self-Help   125

Mall Doors   133

Existing Nail Feng Shui   136

Mashed Potato Time   144

Closer   158

Tonight's Sermon   165

Pierce   173

The Microphone   178

Acknowledgments   189

Your Place in This World

a novella

1.

Your Place in This World

"Tommy, you got a *Bardo*?"

"Washington, Ramirez, Pucinski. Yep, we got him."

A laugh from behind startles Steve. The joy in it reminds him of his mom. He was only four when she died, but he remembers her voice, how playful and musical it was. "Pure country," people used to say. Nothing like the hard Chicago talk—with rocks in the consonants and the threat of throwing them at you in the vowels—that comes out of Ernie and everyone else in the neighborhood.

Steve turns to see a man in tatters mumbling between giggles, searching the walls as if he's lost something there.

"Hey *you*, warming center's down the block. Get moving," the desk sergeant orders.

The laughing man's eyes land on Steve as he makes his way to the door. The two rest their gaze on each other a moment before he sets off to giggling again and walks out of the precinct. Eager to hear more of the joyful laughter, Steve almost follows him.

"Bail is two bills. Got that on you?"

"Yeah," Steve says, pulling a wad from his pocket.

The desk sergeant accepts the rubber-banded roll and eyeballs the boy.

"What's your name, kid?"

"Steve Bardo."

"Let's see some ID. Why aren't you in school, anyways?"

There had been a birth certificate a long time ago. Steve saw it once when he was little. *Baby Boy Bardo*, it said. He thought it was a special document, one just for babies, to show what sex they were. He figured the real one would come when he was older. Truth was his parents never legally named him. He was a full-year-old when his mom saw *Bullitt* starring Steve McQueen and took to calling him after the movie's leading man. Before that, he was either "the kid," or Ernie's favorite—an initialism from the birth certificate—"Triple B," or just "TB."

"I got a pass from the principal," Steve says, handing the sergeant a note written by Ernie's girlfriend, Loraine.

The sergeant reads the bogus letter, shakes his head.

"Which school you go to?"

"Schneider," Steve says, hesitatingly.

"Who's your homeroom teacher?"

"Mr. Napoli."

Within his first month at Schneider, it became clear to Steve's teachers he couldn't keep up with classwork. As such, he'd earned the label "learning disability" and was moved from Mr. Napoli's room to a special class in the basement that didn't have a regular homeroom teacher. A group of different-aged kids—fifth to eighth grade—were in that basement place for special reasons too. Along with the learning disabilities were "bilinguals" who came from foreign countries and "social adjustments" who yelled a lot and threw chairs. Steve understood the bilinguals needed English, but what the rest of them were meant to learn remained a mystery.

"Pull the guy, Tommy," the sergeant says resignedly, returning to his desk and handing the cash to a younger cop.

"Your count is off by three bucks," the younger cop says, flipping through bills.

Steve pretend-searches his pants for the three dollars he'd hoped would go unnoticed. The young cop smiles at the would-be con.

"Gotta find your place in this world, kid. Otherwise, the wrong kinda place'll find you. Catch my drift?"

Steve moves to the window and watches heavy snowfall turn parked cars on Western Ave. into white lumps. A few minutes later, the clang of a metal door announces Ernie's freedom.

"If I see your kid here again, I'm calling family services," the young cop says, marching Ernie into the lobby like the free world is just another, bigger cell that Chicago PD holds the keys to.

"I hear you, officer. I'm going back to A.A. anyways," Ernie says, with a wink aimed at Steve.

Six months earlier, Ernie brought the kid along to the court-ordered meetings. Steve figured the church basement groups were like social adjustments or learning disabilities for grownups. Whatever they were teaching down there didn't take hold for Ernie. But Steve had come to realize something important sitting in the bowels of God's house. There were different floors for different folks, and Ernie and him belonged on the bottom. They were basement people. Not meant to be upstairs praying in the real church, studying in the real school, working in the real office. Coming to this realization brought a certain amount of relief to Steve. For one thing, it stopped him from struggling with homework, trying to get back into Mr. Napoli's class. But what it didn't do was show him how to fit in down there, how to become a good and proper learning disability. Ernie, on the other hand—whether he was "doing hole time" at the state pen, living in a dingy basement "between places," or sitting in the cellar of St. Therese's sipping Twelve-Step coffee—was a bonafide bottom dweller who knew how to engage every aspect of lower-level life.

"I knew you'd come through for the ol' man, Triple B," Ernie says with a canned laugh, steering his son toward the door.

Over time though, Steve began to suspect that nobody really fits in with anybody anywhere in this world. It doesn't matter if they're basement people, upstairs people, or even penthouse people. What gives it away is the struggle, the desperation. The huge effort people put into acting and sounding the same. The maintenance of acceptable words and actions. The tight boundaries they dare not cross lest they be forced to face the reality of their non-belonging. But the most painful part for Steve, the thing that clues him in every time, is the fake laughter.

"Got any cash left?" Ernie asks as they step into the cold.

Steve shakes his head.

"Fuck. I'm dog sick. Loraine's ass better be on the street."

Passing the warming center, Steve runs to the window and looks inside.

"They got coffee and rolls," he says.

"Grab 'em quick, TB. We gotta get moving."

2.

Truth'll Come 'Round

I was looking for refund bottles by the river. Must've had about thirty cents worth by the time I heard Ernie.

"Why dontcha play hooky somewheres I can find 'ya?" He hollered.

I stashed the bottles in a truck tire nearby. For a minute, I thought he was going to make me go to school, like a real dad.

"Come on a-ready," he snapped.

I heard the nerves in his voice and knew—Leon wouldn't front him a bag.

Ernie only panhandled when he was too sick to steal and only dragged me along when his habit was too big to go it alone. It'd been just a few weeks since he got back on stuff, but his jones had already outgrown his ability to turn a buck.

Scuffling up the riverbank, he grabbed my hand and steered us onto Damen, then north toward Belmont, moving us quickly away from the projects so we could find someone hustle-worthy.

"Scuse me, ma'am. Me 'n' my kid got jumped by some *gangbangers* back there. Can ya' help us out?"

I made my sad, scared face like always, and looked into the lady's eyes.

"Shouldn't he be in school?"

"Look at him, lady. The kid's shook'n up. I just wanna buy him a burger and malt over by Gold'n Nugget."

The old lady scrunched her face, turning her drawn-on eyebrows into arrows pointing at her giant schnoz. Probably the biggest one I'd ever seen on a lady. I was sure she was gonna get mad at me for staring, but she pulled her purse close and pinched out a dollar.

"Take care of yourself, *you*," she said, waggling the bill in front of me.

I said, "Thank you," kind of stony. I didn't like her telling me what to do.

Ernie was a fast walker and even faster talker. By the time we got to the El stop at Irving and Sheridan, we must've made seven bucks. Below the tracks, three Ricans in tank tops and baggy slacks were leaning against the brick wall of the train entrance. They seemed to recognize Ernie, or at least recognize his jones. They nodded as we walked up. Ernie chin-jutted at the middle-sized one, like Goldilocks might do if she were a junkie. When Ernie and the guy disappeared around the corner to do the deal, one of the brick-leaners told me to move away.

"It's a free country," I said.

"Knuckle sane-wish free today too, *punk*," he said, waving a lazy fist.

I walked around the corner and looked in the gangway. Ernie was lying on the ground groaning.

"I got beat," he said.

When I got Ernie on his feet, he pulled a stashed dollar out of his sock and blew it on train fare. Ernie hated paying for the CTA, but he was too sick to jump turnstiles and run.

"Sucker punch," he said, as the train left daylight, rattling down into the subway. "Truth'll come 'round on that punk."

We switched for the O'Hare line downtown and rode to Wicker Park. Not seeing anyone he knew on the street, Ernie walked us around the corner. I recognized the gold and black Latin King colors on the young guys. Some of them made gang signs, hand crowns, when cars drove by.

We came to a brick three-flat at the end of the block and entered a vestibule. Ernie never brought me in close when he copped, so I wasn't sure what was going on. After he rang the bell, a skinny, sweaty guy came downstairs and answered. His eyes were bugging out like Ernie's did when he shot speedballs.

"Need a sixteent', bro," Ernie said.

The guy spit a baggie out of his mouth. While Ernie pretend-searched his pocket for money, he slipped me the baggie and whispered, "*Run.*"

Before I could think what to do, the skinny guy reached into a built-in wall mailbox and pulled out a kitchen knife. He had it at Ernie's throat in a split second. I tossed the dope at his feet.

"*Be cool*, Julio," Ernie said, raising his hands.

We backed out of the building and ran in the opposite direction of the Latin Kings. The ones Julio was hollering at.

On the way home, we made a lot more money panhandling. It was obvious Ernie was telling the truth that time. I wasn't hurt too bad, but my glasses were broken again.

When we got near Lathrop Homes, I went back down to the river. I could see good enough to find the tire where my bottles were stashed, but not good enough to hunt for more.

Ernie caught up with me later, when I was coming out of Nino's with thirty cents' worth of Sugar Babies and Alexander the Grape.

"TB," he grunted, handing over my glasses with the frames re-taped.

I knew he was well again. Even before seeing his eyes.

"Get a burger and malt over by Gold'n Nugget," he told me, stuffing two dollars in my pocket.

I went by Junior's and got a polish and fries instead, pocketing the extra dollar for the movies. I hated people telling me what to do. Especially Ernie.

3.

Liberty Bell

Ernie pulled a paper ticket out of a machine, handed it to me, and chin-jutted toward the back of the room. I dragged myself over there and found a seat. It was easier to focus on faces past the low wooden gate than the ones nearby.

"I ain't s'posed to do more papers. I given y'all that last time. I need my *check*."

"If you want a check this month, bring proper documentation by end of day," the office lady said, talking over the complaining woman's shoulder as if warding off an evil spirit just to the left and behind her.

The scrappy back and forth about paperwork, IDs, and dollar amounts made the overhead fluorescents glow brighter. A bailiff squinted at the desk.

"Bitch, *please*," the angry mother said, snatching a document from the welfare worker's hand and dragging her little boy back to the waiting side.

The wooden gate separating the government side from the waiting side was nothing compared to the wall behind the welfare lady's face. For people like us, the ones on the waiting side, she was no different than cops, judges, teachers, bondsmen, or any other authority type we needed to vent on. You could yell forever and never get past that wall.

When our number was nearly up, I went to the bathroom to find Ernie. I walked past smokers and urinal pissers toward the sit-down toilets. The stall doors had been removed to stop bad things from happening inside. It didn't. In the first stall was an old man doubled over a seatless crapper, grunting and crying. In the next one, a man in ragged clothes was arguing with a woman who wasn't there—or maybe he was practicing for later. In the third stall, a tall skinny guy was yanking on his thing with both hands like he was trying to rip it off his body. I tried not to look, but I did. It was the biggest thing I'd ever seen. In the last stall, the one I knew I'd find him in, Ernie was slumped back with one eyelid cracked open. *At least he put his funny gun away*, I thought.

"Number's up," I said.

"Gotta be kidding me. I just got here," Ernie said.

It'd been thirty-five minutes, but Ernie didn't understand time the way other people did, the way a clock did.

"Fifty-one, *last chance*," the bailiff said.

"Fifty-one!" I yelled as we turned the corner.

The bailiff pointed to a desk.

"Ernest Bardo?" The welfare lady asked the space behind Ernie.

"Present," Ernie said with a gravelly chuckle.

When we were almost back to Lathrop Homes, Ernie handed me a sixty-five-dollar book of food stamps. It was the first time I'd noticed the Liberty Bell on its cover. In Social Studies, we were reading about American independence. The teacher said we were free to live as we wanted because we had fought hard for that right.

"Why's the Liberty Bell cracked?" I asked Ernie.

"Same reason people are cracked," he said, chin-jutting toward Nino's bodega.

I walked inside and handed the fresh book of stamps to Nino. He looked past me through the window and popped the register.

"I keepin' the five he owe," Nino said, handing me forty-seven in cash—the usual eighty cents on the dollar minus Ernie's five. I put a dollar in my pocket before walking out.

"That pork chop bastard beat you," Ernie grunted, counting the cash.

"You owed him six."

"I'll crack *him* like the fuckin' Liberty Bell," Ernie threatened half-heartedly, hustling toward the dopespot.

I rode the El downtown to catch a triple feature at The Oriental. After paying the dollar entrance, I pushed past people 'til I saw the broken middle-row seat with a split running up its back. I was glad to find it empty, even though it usually was. I sat down, fidgeting the grooves in the armrest where I had carved and re-carved my initials so many times, waiting for the lights to dim, waiting for the people to disappear.

4.

Pick a Part

Ernie came around the foster home saying he needed my help. It was a school day. Mrs. Williams said if I missed any more of seventh grade they'd send me to The Audy Home, but she said a lot of goofy stuff when she was drinking. One time she even claimed to be my real mom.

"That's the voice of cheap vodka right there," Ernie'd said.

I still remembered Mom. She definitely wasn't Mrs. Williams.

I asked, "Where we going again?"

"Boneyard, Slim," he said, as we stepped into a busted-up van.

It was funny being called Slim. I guess it sounded more grown-up than "Kid" or "Triple B." But less personal, like I was any old sidekick.

We pulled into the parking lot, which already looked like a boneyard. He pointed at the sign.

"*U Pull It*. Named after your favorite pastime."

He made that canned corn laugh that always hurt my ears.

"It says Pick a Part. U Pull It is the other place," I told him.

He said, "Guess all that pullin' improved your eyesight, Slim. Goes the other way for me." Then he did the corny laugh again.

The office guy was wearing blue coveralls with a name patch sewn on. Ernie wanted to know which way to a '71 LeSabre.

"What do you need off it?"

"Not much," Ernie said.

The office guy pointed a finger and went back to reading the paper.

We walked in that direction a long time. The snow was up to my knees. It looked like those rows of rusty cars went on forever.

Ernie said, "I could spot a LeSabre a mile away."

I was getting cold.

He told me, "You carry the goods, I'll buy you a burrito the size of your arm."

I already figured that.

Ernie got to work pulling parts. I got behind the wheel, pretend-driving away from Chicago like always. I felt around the seats for change. Didn't find any. Opened the glove box. Empty too. Got out and popped the trunk with a screwdriver and hammer the way Ernie showed me one time.

Just the usual stuff. Tire and jack. Rags. Half-full quarts of oil.

But there was an envelope poking out from under the spare. That was funny to me. I tried pulling, but it was stuck pretty good, and I didn't want to tear it. I was thinking it might have something important inside like cash or a ransom note.

After I got the spare moved, there was more grease on me than Ernie. I wiped my hands on my pants trying not to smudge the envelope. There was just one piece of paper inside, the kind with lines like you use in school. The lady's handwriting was nice.

Dearest Tom,

You can say whatever you want, but I will always be yours. And no matter what you think, the baby is yours too. I don't know what happened or why. And I don't care what Jimmy or anybody else told you. Oh, but I wish you still had even a crumb of care for me. I love love love you. Is there any reason to live other than to be with you? I hope hope hope you get this before something bad happens. Please don't forget us. Please don't let something bad happen.
Yours forever and ever,
Stacy

Ernie called me over and said, "Take this linkage and that rod."

I had to put the long metal part down my pant leg. It made me walk stiff like I had a cast on. I was sure the office guy would notice. Ernie told me to keep moving while he paid for some cheap part. I walked to the van quick, not so much afraid of being caught, but I thought if I looked, the office guy's name patch was going to say Tom, like in the letter.

We got big burritos at El Ranchero after, and then went to fix the LeSabre. I handed Ernie tools and sipped his Old Style when he wasn't looking. He joked about his beer evaporating. After a while, I got more bold and took a whole tall boy for myself. Then another one. Ernie was busy wrenching and didn't notice or didn't care. He was a good mechanic when he stayed off stuff. At least that's what Mrs. Williams said.

When I felt the beer in me, I climbed inside the trunk and lay there watching the garage roof spin. Ernie woke me later and carried me to the van. It was really freezing out then. I rubbed my jacket on the window and saw a guy pay him for wrenching on the LeSabre.

On the way back to the foster home, Ernie said he needed to make a stop. I knew it was the West Side by the abandoned houses. Some were half burned down. It was like a boneyard for buildings instead of cars. He ran inside one and came out quick. I knew he was fixing in the back of the van, so I didn't look. When it got quiet, I climbed over the seats and shook him, saying it was time to go.

He opened his eyes a little and said, "Yeah? Well, you got drunk on beer."

He was too high to do the corny laugh.

Ernie didn't come around much after that. I guess he stopped wrenching on cars.

For a long time, I kept the envelope in a tobacco can under my bed at Mrs. Williams's place. I'd pull it out and read it once in a while. Usually just a sentence or two. Sometimes I wondered what she looked like, or what Jimmy said, or if something bad did happen. Sometimes I wondered if I should put the letter back where I found it.

5.

Blue Man

I could hear Loraine hollering. It must've been five in the morning.

"You spent the money on *what?*"

I peeked my head out the door and saw Ernie waving his hands slowly.

"Hear me out, babe. They were a steal."

"Where you even find sump'n like that?"

"Leon hooked me up," Ernie croaked, tossing her a baggie of brown powder. "Babe, you know what today is, dontcha?"

"Yeah, it's the day I stop giving money to a fool who blows it on *jigaboo* cream," Loraine screeched, catching the dope with one hand, reaching for her cooker with the other.

"Today's Sunday, babe. Maxwell Street," Ernie said, pulling a can of Murray's Pomade out of a box.

"This et'nic hair care product sells for a buck and a quarter by Woolwort's. I'm 'onna sell 'em for fifty cents a pop. Each box got a *hunnerd* in it. That's fifty a box right there, babe. And check this, I got two boxes off Leon. Only ten bucks each."

Loraine found the least infected vein in her foot and registered. Her screech dropped an octave when the dope hit.

"Fuck off, Ern. You got beat by a cheat," she said.

"Me 'n the Kid are gonna hawk 'em. You'll see."

"Hey Kid… Steve…"

Ernie only called me Steve when he really needed something.

I usually ran off before he roped me into one of his sideways scams. But I wanted to see Maxwell Street again, and me and Ernie hadn't hung out much since I moved back from the foster home. Plus, he had wheels now, so I knew we wouldn't be hoofing it or taking the CTA.

In the car, I thought about the times Ernie had taken me to Maxwell Street as a little kid, to help sell cameras, radios, tools, and other crap that, for whatever reason, he had a hard time fencing in the neighborhood. He always said it was like Disneyland for people into stolen stuff and blues.

"This is where every great bluesman got started," he told me the first time we went.

I thought he was saying "blue man." It made me think of how he looked when I found him OD'd in a gas station bathroom one time.

We parked on South Halsted and popped the trunk. Ernie put a box up on his shoulder and handed me a can of Murray's to wave around. We waded through the crowd of shoppers and street people, past vendors at sawhorse tables piled with every kind of junk for sale, while he hollered, "Murray's *Palm-Aid*! Et'nic hair cares! Fifty cents only! Don't get robbed by the pharmacy slob!"

The hair grease was selling so fast, I had to hold onto six or seven cans at a time. I think we sold a whole box in an hour.

After the first box, we took a break and went by Jim's Original for breakfast. Ernie had a pork chop sandwich and a half-pint of Wild Irish Rose. I had two polishes with fries and two cans of RC.

"Loraine knows her per'fession, but she don't know nuttin' about real entrepreneur-shit," he burped, as we finished our food and got up from the curb.

When we went back to it, I started pocketing quarters, knowing that by the time Ernie added up his profits, he'd lose count from blowing money every-which-way. Halfway through selling the second box, I heard music coming from around a corner. It was blues I guess, but really different from what other musicians played around Maxwell Street. I ran over to check it out.

In a dirt lot, near a pile of bricks and worn-out tires, a grey-haired Black man sat on two milk crates, singing into an old-timey microphone duct-taped to a metal rod. His faded red guitar looked like it was plugged into a space heater. The sound echoed around the crumbling tenements bordering the lot, bouncing hard off bricks and hitting me in the head and chest. It was the saddest music I'd ever heard. When he finished the song, I went over to ask his name. Sounded like he said, "Dirty Nugget." I put eight quarters and a can of Murray's in his guitar case.

He said, "God gwanna bless ya' bwah."

It was the weirdest accent I'd ever heard. I couldn't imagine where he came from to sing and talk like that.

Ernie called me over. I wanted to stay and listen. He said the cans were all sold, and it was time to go.

"Do they play Dirty Nugget on the radio?" I asked, flipping around the FM dial in Ernie's beat-up Nova.

He said, "Go to the lie berry. They got plenny albums on them old blues cats."

Ernie was too busy flooring it to the dopespot to notice the quarters stuffed in my pockets, shoes, and socks. I kept them spread apart so none of them looked too bulky. But it was Loraine you had to worry about. She had a sixth sense for sniffing out stashed cash, especially when she was sick.

When we got back to Lathrop Homes, I went off to my secret spot—a truck tire by the Chicago River—to count my quarters. Eight dollars and seventy-five cents in total. It was the most I'd had all at once since nabbing a sawbuck from Mrs. Williams's shoebox two months earlier—the exact reason I got sent back to Ernie in the first place. I was going to use that stolen tenner to catch a train to somewhere far from Chicago. Until I saw Dirty Nugget, that is. After hearing him, it seemed like Maxwell Street was already somewhere far away from Chicago. I hid the quarters in my tobacco can and buried it under the tire.

The next day, I took some of my stash and caught the El to State and Randolph, the same stop I usually got off to go to The Oriental Theater. But I wasn't interested in movies that day. I was going to the downtown library.

I walked up to a desk and asked where I could find Dirty Nugget's albums. The librarian said she didn't know that "band" and pointed me to where they kept the rock records. I wondered how she could think a famous bluesman was a rock band.

There were rows of records labeled by different styles—rock, pop, jazz, folk, country, classical—but none of them said blues. I pulled out random records and listened to them with headsets. Some sounded like radio music or stuff from old movies. A lot of it was really boring. I probably spent two hours digging through all that junk before I figured out blues was mixed up in the jazz section, which made no sense.

The blues singers all had funny names. I liked some of them. Howlin' Wolf, Lightnin' Hopkins, Blind Boy Fuller. But I didn't see Dirty Nugget. I figured he must be so famous his records were already checked out. I was about to give up and go catch the triple feature at The Oriental, but then I saw his picture on the front of a record. It was called *Peoples*

Always Dyin' by Diggy Nubbit. I listened to it ten times in a row, straight.

When the library was getting ready to close, I copied the album's liner notes onto scrap paper the librarian gave me.

Alonzo Thompson, who became known as Diggy Nubbit, was born in Issaquena, Mississippi around 1915.

While it is believed that Nubbit performed under several aliases in the 1930s, his earliest known recordings (not presented here) were in 1947 for the short-lived Jackson, Mississippi-based Surefire Records label. Rumor had it that Nubbit proved to be a bad omen for Surefire which went out of business just prior to the release of Nubbit's two sides "Deepen your Grave" and "Sweet Red Dirt." Oddly, this trend continued for Nubbit throughout his career. Memphis-based Ron-Jon Records folded after a Nubbit recording in 1951, as did St. Louis' Sugarbowl Records immediately following a Nubbit session in 1954.

By the time he arrived in Chicago in 1956, word had spread of 'Bad Luck Nubbit.' No record label would touch him, and few venues would host his performance. Unable to earn his living as a bluesman, Nubbit instead settled for work as a gravedigger, hence the moniker, Diggy. The title of this album states Peoples Always Dyin' — that fundamental human truth has been the basis of Nubbit's income for the majority of his life.

During the 1960s American Folk Music revival, a few enthusiastic college students resolved to preserve Diggy's work, resulting in this collection of Nubbit nuggets. Coincidentally, the students responsible for producing these recordings flunked out of their respective University programs immediately following the recording of this disc, further adding to the 'Bad Luck Nubbit' legend.

As to Nubbit's performance style, his singing is reminiscent of the high falsetto of Skip James or John Jacob Niles and yet also the guttural booming of Blind Willie Johnson and Howlin' Wolf. This back-and-forth between opposite vocal techniques gives his voice a shapeshifting quality, sounding almost as if two people were performing at once and from very different perspectives. There is also a distinctive tuning to Nubbit's "one strang fo' each finger" five string guitar—uncommon for American blues and more akin to the West African xalam (in this writer's opinion)—which adds a mysterious and ancient quality to the music. Lyrically, his songs share in common blues themes such as love-gone-wrong, sex, violence, hard labor, death, and drinking, but Diggy's vocal phrasing is so unusual, that verse and chorus often seem out of sequence, as if sung backward or inside out. There is little mathematical rhyme or reason to be found in Nubbit's poetry either. Nothing of the twelve-bar blues here.

Fellow Mississippi bluesman Ishy 'Kingbee' Davis once said of Nubbit: "His music too damn freaky. Too sad. Most sad even for the blues." This characterization can certainly be found on the ten tracks presented here. The small group of us who have come to appreciate the dark poetry and peculiar melancholy of Nubbit's music, think it best to warn listeners of the gut-wrenching nature of these recordings. The music is in fact so mournful, it is not recommended for the lone listener, particularly if one harbors a depressive disposition. Generally speaking, the daylight hours may not well withstand a spinning of this disc.

Today, Nubbit can be found haunting Chicago's Maxwell Street Market, where he continues to perform his original, odd, and otherworldly tunes for passersby on Sundays just before daybreak.

I read the liner notes over and over on the El ride home. It was exciting to know more about Diggy, but it felt like I knew too much. Like the part about his real name, Alonzo. It sounded like a clown's name. Like Bozo, but for a clown who was all alone. Alone-zo the Clown. That's what they'll call me if I ever join the circus, I thought.

I had a burger and malt by Golden Nugget before going home, probably because it sounded like Diggy Nubbit. His songs were still echoing around like they did in the dirt lot off Maxwell Street, only instead of brick walls, they were bouncing inside my head and chest. Especially "Whistlin' Shotgun."

Whistlin' shotgun. Stairs don't end
Whistlin' shotgun. Stairs go down.
Whistlin' whistlin'. Too many peoples
Whistlin' shotgun. Babies in the ground.
Babies in the ground. Babies in the ground.
Whistlin' shotgun. Babies in the ground.

Nobody was home when I got there. I was relieved about that. I took our little black and white Panasonic with its coat hanger antenna and slipped into my room. Like everything else in our apartment, the TV was too beat up to pawn or sell. I watched an old movie on WGN starring Peter Lorry. His bugged-out eyes made you think he'd been shooting speedballs.

I was falling asleep when Loraine came in. You could always tell when she was home. A lot of bangs and slams to let you know it. She pushed my door open hard.

"Your dumbfuck dad blew his wad and nearly kilt hisself!" She hollered. Her heavy makeup was smeared.

"Is he ok?" I asked.

"Is *he* ok? Nobody ever asks if *I'm* ok!" She screamed, slamming the door. I went out to the living room and waited for her to say something else. She started crying then.

"I found the asshole near dead in the bathroom. Three empty balloons laying next to him. They was them hope-to-die bags from the West Side. And he didn't even save me *one*! His chump ass was so blue he was purple…"

"Where's he now?" I asked.

"County."

"Jail or hospital?"

"Oh, *he'll* be alright. He'll be just fine and dandy. But I'm sick and tired. And now I gotta go out and trick in this shitty weather!"

I figured she meant county hospital. If he were in jail she would've sent me back to Mrs. Williams already.

In my room, I imagined Diggy singing "Whistlin' Shotgun" while shoveling dirt over Ernie. Loraine was there, wearing a black veil to cover her smeary makeup. Alone-zo the Clown walked around with big funny shoes and a red nose, passing out West Side balloons to all the dopefiends who came to pay respects.

When Ernie got home the next morning, he was still wearing a Cook County Hospital wristband.

"Junkie jewelry," he laughed when I mentioned it.

I went down by the river and re-read Diggy's liner notes. From then on, I called my secret spot "Issaquena" after his hometown.

6.

Chump Day

"My name's Ernie."

When it was clear he wasn't going to say "and" like everybody else, a guy one seat over started talking.

"I'm Lenny, and I'm and attic, and I still got stinkin' thinkin'…"

"And, and, and…*these fools sure can gripe*," Ernie whispered to me.

"…and when it comes to fambly, that's youse in this room. Cuz my addiction's out there doing pushups in the parkin' lot. And youse know, like I do, the normies and square johns just don't get it."

When it was over, everyone held hands and chanted the usual words. It was like Pledge of Allegiance, except their eyes were closed. Like they were trying to keep something from getting in. I figured it was their addiction they were shutting out, like that guy Lenny was saying. Ernie was the only one with his eyes open during the chanting. He didn't have to worry about his habit coming back since it never left.

Ernie went to get his court paper signed by a guy sitting with books and pamphlets all around him. I went to the percolator, poured a quarter cup of cream powder and sugar in a styrofoam cup, and squirted in enough coffee to make it hot.

"Keep coming back!" The pamphlet guy hollered as we walked out of the church.

"Keep coming back, my ass. Bunch of snivelers. See, that's how they make you join 'em. You get bored *to tears*," Ernie said, laughing at his own joke.

"I liked it," I said.

"For what? Not that crappy coffee."

"Some of them guys got chips for being clean a long time."

"Don't be a chump, kid. Nickels to nails they're still half in the bag. That Lenny clown more than any of 'em. But most are pretenders, weekend warriors at best. They ain't got it in 'em to be bonafides."

Bonafides was Ernie lingo for true dope fiends, like him and Loraine.

"Merry Christmas Eve," one of the Twelve-Steppers said when we got out to the parking lot.

"See that. A real junkie don't get no holidays. Ought to call it *Chump Day Eve*," Ernie said as we climbed into the Nova and peeled out.

To Ernie, everyone was either a chump or a bonafide.

The snow was coming down hard. I could barely see out of the windshield, but I knew where we were going.

"Where are those fuckers?" Ernie said, beating on the wheel as we slid through the bombed-out streets between Washington and Jackson on the West Side.

I knew better than to talk when Ernie was sick, but I was thinking about the dealers too. Were they chumps or bonafides? I worried they were chumps, sitting in warm apartments, eating big dinners, laughing, opening presents—like in the movies—instead of out here in the streets with the bonafides, ready to make Ernie well again.

We were cruising slow down a side street when Ernie spotted a young black dude coming out of a gangway.

"My man, where the *slingers*?" Ernie yelled out the window.

"Souls and Vice Lords mixed it up today. Po-lice been heavy in these streets. Look here, I can get whatchoo need…"

Ernie sized the guy up and drove off before he got close. A couple blocks later, I heard gunshots, then sirens.

"They're playing my song," Ernie said, with a cracked laugh.

"Why don't you score off Leon?" I asked, hoping he would turn us around and buy the drugs by our place.

"That sawdust? Nah. Been stepped on by too many a' Santa's helpers," he said.

When we got near Madison and California, Ernie finally saw someone he knew.

"Get behind the wheel, kid," he said.

I slid across the bench seat while he got out to score. I was big enough to reach the foot pedals by then. While Ernie disappeared into a building, I revved the engine hard a couple times, imagining I was about to peel out like a getaway driver in the movies.

"Don't be wasting gas," Ernie scolded, scooting me over and swatting my head. He wanted to fix in the car, but there were too many cops circling the area.

Driving up Clybourn, near the projects, we saw Loraine in her work outfit—stiletto shoes, fake fur coat, mini-skirt—dragging a small Christmas tree behind her.

"Fuck is she doing?" Ernie asked.

"Bout time. Hurry up. We gotta decorate!" Loraine shouted staccato-like. I could tell by her fast-paced talking she'd been smoking coke again.

I helped her get the tree in the apartment while Ernie ran to the bathroom. Lorraine cooked Jiffy Pop on a hotplate while barking orders at me.

"Scissors. Magazines. Needle and thread!"

When the popcorn was done, she threaded it all together and wrapped it around the tree. I cut pieces of magazine paper into stars and hung those too. Ernie came out and landed heavy on the couch.

"You're gonna make the kid think he's getting a present," he groaned.

"I got sumpin' for youse *both*," Loraine chirped, placing two tinfoil-wrapped packages under the tree.

"And you better have sumpin' for me, *Ernest*," she said greedily.

Ernie pulled a little balloon from his pocket and flicked it toward her with his thumb. Lorraine snatched it mid-air, catlike.

The first time I saw those brightly-colored balloons, we were learning nation flags at school. Ernie left some sitting on top of the steamer trunk we called a coffee table while he was looking for his works. Three little balloons—yellow, green, and red. Just like the flags of Congo, Cameroon, and Ethiopia. When I opened one, I found a black ball in wax paper. It gave off a strong scent. Kind of vinegary. I figured it must have come all the way from Africa.

While Loraine ran to the bathroom with her balloon, I picked up the gift marked *Steven*. She knew my name was just Steve, not "Steven," but she called me that when she wanted to pretend I was someone different than the kid she hated. I peeled off the thin layer of tin foil and was stoked when I saw it was a little boom box—a Sanyo single-speaker two band radio cassette player. It was beat all to hell, but when I plugged it in it worked just fine.

"Prolly lifted it off one of her chumps..." Ernie croaked.

Ever on the listen for someone talking bad about her, Loraine poked her head around the corner just then.

"Yeah? Well, I happen to know you stole silverwares from an ol' lady to buy all that skag *you* been pigging out on lately, so don't be the judge of me, Ernie!" She yammered, slamming the door for emphasis.

It was my first radio. I didn't care if it was stolen. I flipped around the channels like I did in the car. Most of the stations were just people talking—politics, religion, sports—or else they played corny stuff like "Afternoon Delight" and "How Deep is Your Love." But then I found one with an announcer whose voice was echoing in a funny way. He said:

"From down in the basement with his giant *economy*-sized orange crate, WNIB proudly presents the *Big Bill Collins Show*."

I got excited when the music came on. The records Big Bill was spinning sounded a lot like the blues and soul I'd heard on Maxwell Street. Big Bill gave a phone number so you could call in and make a request. I really wanted to call, but we didn't have a phone. I was hoping he would play my favorite Maxwell Street bluesman, Diggy Nubbit, but he didn't. Still, I had a line to the outside world, the blues world, and that was something.

The next morning, Ernie told me to go by the church and get some free toys. I was too old to play with toys, but I knew what he meant. Loraine wanted me to get lost. I went by the church anyway and nabbed some milky coffee and a sweet roll. That guy Lenny from the Twelve-Step group was there, handing out junky Woolworth's stuff like plastic army men and generic baby dolls. I walked up behind him and saw a five-years-clean Narcotics Anonymous chip dangling off his key ring. He didn't look "half in the bag" to me.

It wasn't too cold out, so I started walking. When I got to Clybourn and Halsted, I realized I was heading south. I guess my feet knew I was going to Maxwell Street before I did. It was Sunday, market day, but it was Christmas too. I didn't know if anything would be happening down there or not.

When I got to Maxwell Street, there were a handful of people selling stuff and others wandering around dressed up, like they'd just come from church. I went by the dirt lot where I'd seen Diggy Nubbit play a couple months earlier, but he wasn't around. Nobody else was either. I walked between the broke-down tenements and stood right where his milk crate chair had been. And then I did something funny. I'm not sure why, but I started singing Diggy's song "Whistlin' Shotgun." I closed my eyes and imagined I was really him. "Bad Luck Nubbit." All the way from Issaquena, Mississippi. The world's saddest bluesman. Pretty soon, I was clapping and singing at the same time.

When I finished the song, I heard applause. I opened my eyes, and in front me, standing there, were two old Black ladies, a Mexican family, and a few wino types. The Mexican dad gave some coins to a little girl dressed in a frilly outfit. She came over shyly and dropped them by my feet. One of the old ladies flashed a gold tooth smile and handed me some quarters. The other one said, "Go 'head, sing yo' song child," and gave me a dollar bill.

Even one of the winos tossed a little change. I felt embarrassed for singing in that strong Issaquena accent, pretending to be Diggy.

I caught the El back instead of walking, feeling the money in one pant's pocket and Lenny's five-year chip in the other. It seemed like Loraine should get a Christmas present too, but I wasn't about to blow my singing money on her. In the end, I swiped her some Hostess mini donuts from Nino's. I was no chump.

7.

Disguises

No one cared what the substitute teacher had to say, but I liked her voice. It was light and lispy. She said it was the first day of Spring. The dirty snow piled up outside told another story. On the blackboard, she spelled out her name, Miss Petuli—like a cross between a petunia and a tulip—and then wrote which chapters we were supposed to read, chapters about the Civil War. I thumbed through the textbook's scribbled-on pages, the handiwork of earlier eighth graders, histories easier to follow than the ones I was meant to read. It was all the usual stuff Chicago kids fill in anywhere there's a blank space. Gang signs, like crosses, crowns, pyramids, five-point stars, six-point stars, right-side-up pitchforks, upside-down pitchforks, dice, playing cards. And nicknames sketched out in boxy, old English letters, like Lil' Stoner, Smiley, P'fessor, Froggy, Joker—some with a RIP written next to them. And, of course, endless doodles. Kilroys, cubes, spirals, all-seeing-eyes, cartoon characters, and lots and lots of dicks, pussies, and tits. Running through all of it were declarations of love and hate, though for sure less love and more hate, especially between the Latin Kings and Insane Deuces. They were having their own mini-Civil War right there at George Schneider Elementary.

When the bell rang, I went to my secret spot down by the river and made a little fire. I stood there trying to keep warm, wolfing down the sandwiches and tot-sized cartons of chocolate milk I swiped from the lunchroom. The wind kept blowing smoke in my face like it was laughing at me for making a lame fire. Loraine wasn't living with us anymore, so at least I didn't have to worry about her raging mood swings when I went home. Ernie said she moved in with one of her chumps. I never saw her around Lathrop after that.

On the way to the apartment, I walked the long way around a clique of Deuces decked out in green and black—just juniors and peewees, but they were always more trouble than the older bangers. A quarter block past them, rocks were still cracking on the sidewalk around me. The rock-chuckers were yelling "represent," and "Deuce 'hood." I didn't throw hand signs or call out a gang name since I didn't belong to one. They called me a pussy when I picked up my pace. I knew if I fought them, the big Deuces would come around real quick.

There were two empty narc cars parked on our block when I got there. By the light dusting of snow on them, I could tell they hadn't been there long. Probably busting that small-time dealer, Leon, I thought. When I got closer, I saw a couple plainclothesmen push a man in cuffs out the door. It was Ernie. I jumped around a corner and watched from there. The narcs shoved him in back of one of the rides, a brand new '81 Crown Vic, bumping his head hard on the way in. I heard Ernie yell something. Probably, "Fuck."

When they left, I stared at the spots where the cars had been, as if the oil-stained snow might explain what happened. But I knew already.

Walking inside the building, I found our apartment door hanging open. The cops had busted the chain link, tearing the screws out of the door jamb. I listened for a minute before locking the deadbolt behind me. The place was a mess. I couldn't tell if it was the usual kind or the upshot of a police scuffle. The first thing I did was check under my bed. It was a relief to find my boombox there. The black-and-white Panasonic with its broken dial and coat hanger antenna was still in my room too. I sat there a long time, watching news and reruns on WGN, the only station that came in clear.

I went to the icebox when I got hungry, though I knew there wouldn't be much. A can of Old Style, a half stick of butter, and a near-empty bottle of hot sauce were the only things not rotten. In a cupboard, I found a hardened jar of instant coffee, an old bag of rice, a can of navy beans, some flour, and a little brown sugar in a Tupperware. I knew how to cook that stuff and make it taste like something.

I ate the rice and beans with my poor man's shortbread while watching the late movie. It was called *The Story of Dr. Wassell*. One of those old, boring war movies where they make some guy out to be a big hero. Night Beat with Marty McNeeley came on after that. Marty was talking about the CIA and the Russians and someplace below Mexico. More war stuff. That got me wondering if I could fake my age and join the army. I'd seen disguise kits for sale at Curiosity Corner, a novelty shop over by Broadway and Melrose. I figured that would do the trick.

The next morning, I checked Ernie's drawers and secret stash spots for anything valuable. In his leather jacket, I found a crumpled five-dollar food stamp stuck in the lining where the pocket had blown out. I took it to Nino's bodega and bought some eggs, bread, milk, and candy.

Back in the apartment, I moved the TV around and messed with the antenna until I tuned in a station with Saturday morning cartoons. Thundarr the Barbarian came in real fuzzy like it was sprinkled with dirty snow. That was ok for me, it matched how I was feeling. I ate egg sandwiches with the last of the hot sauce and watched people dance on *Soul Train* when the cartoons ended.

I kept an ear aimed at the door all day but never heard the rustle of Ernie's keys. Pretty soon, it was getting dark. I started wishing Loraine would come around, even though I didn't like her almost as much as she didn't like me. At least then someone could tell me if Ernie was going to bond out or not.

When I got sick of watching TV, I flipped around the dials on my boombox. I found a foreign language station and stayed there for a bit, pretending the voices were coming from aliens in outer space. At two a.m., I tuned into WNIB for the overnight blues show. The way Big Bill Collins, the deejay, talked always cheered me up. I fell asleep listening to him.

In the morning, I finished the last of the eggs and bread with some milky instant coffee. It was a lot warmer outside, and the dirty snow was melting fast. Seemed like a good chance to scavenge for coins and other treasures that'd been buried all winter.

Down the block, I ran into a dopefiend called Gigs, short for Gigglesnort. He told me Ernie got busted for B and E and was for sure going back to the pen. I knew Ernie'd been stealing more than usual by all the weird doodads lying around the apartment. Ugly little statues, plates, and candleholders—stuff he couldn't fence, I guess. Ernie stole more boldly when his habit got big, pulling jobs in broad daylight, sometimes even on our own block. Before Loraine left, before Ernie started robbing everybody blind, she called him "half a chili pimp" and said she wasn't going to pay his way anymore. I guess you couldn't blame her for what happened, but I did.

I left Gigs and started walking east, scouring the ground for silver coins in the evaporating slush. I hit up a couple laundromats too, they were usually good for a few lost dimes under the machines.

After pulling a little change together, I decided to go to Maxwell Street since it was Sunday. I paid the El fare, though I probably should've jumped the turnstile and used the money for food. Soon as I got off the train, I ran past the hawkers, shoppers, and brown-bag day-drinkers 'til I was way out at the edge of the market.

And then I heard it, heard him.

I worried it might just be a boombox bouncing his music off the buildings, but he was there alright—sitting on two stacked-up milk crates, singing and picking his guitar. Diggy Nubbit, the world's saddest bluesman.

There was no one but me and him in that muddy patch of dirt all morning. It was like my own private concert. After I'd been watching a while, he waved me over.

"Ain't got no other chil'rens to play with?" He asked.

I said I was nearly fourteen, that I wasn't a child. When he didn't say anything else, I told him I liked his song, "Whistlin' Shotgun."

"Whatchoo know about *Whistlin' Shotgun*?" He asked.

I must've listened to his album a hundred times at the downtown library. I knew the names and words to every song. He played "Whistlin' Shotgun" for me, and I mouthed along. When he finished, he said I could pass the hat for him if I wanted to. It was funny, him asking me to do that when no one else was there. Of course, I walked around with the hat anyway. I was just happy to be with him.

People did start coming after that. Probably because they saw me waving his upside-down fedora out, begging style. At the end of the morning, when Diggy counted the hat money, there was more than ten dollars in change. He gave me four quarters and told me to come back the next Sunday.

I walked the whole way home, flipping quarters, reading the print dates, imagining they were magic, like Jack and the Beanstalk beans. I waited long as I could, maybe three hours, before blowing the money on peanut butter and saltines at Nino's.

That next week, I stayed home school days, ducking cops and truant officers, only going out nights and weekends to scavenge returnable bottles and re-up on food. I kept thinking Ernie would come back, or maybe a teacher or welfare worker would come around, but they didn't. The only knock that whole time was the super letting me know they were turning the water off for a day while they fixed something.

I couldn't wait for Sunday to roll around so I could see Diggy again. His songs cheered me up even though they were mostly about death and other sad stuff. But it wasn't just the music, I liked being there, being part of something. He was pretty quiet when he wasn't singing, though. Sometimes he'd look at you like he was saying something without saying it. I got the feeling he knew my dad was in the pen and that I was living alone.

A week went by and another week after that. Still no sign of Ernie. Maybe I should've missed him more than I did. I definitely felt bad for him being locked up and all but figured at least he was on the other side of the kick by then. For me, even though it was boring staying in watching TV all day, it was still a lot easier than going around Schneider and dealing with the bangers and all their bullshit. Most of all, I knew Diggy would be waiting for me when Sunday rolled around. That was more than enough to keep me going.

At the end of each Sunday afternoon, Diggy counted the cash I collected and, no matter how much we made, handed me back four quarters. I started pinching the pot when he wasn't looking, figuring I needed the money more than he did. And anyway, he probably wouldn't've made so much if it wasn't for me wagging his old, beat-up hat around all day.

It was going pretty good for a while, until one Sunday when I got to the lot a little later than usual. Diggy didn't say anything about it, but when he handed me his hat, he gave a cold look with his eyes and mouth. The first number he sang that morning, "By the Thumbs," was about an innocent man being tortured for stealing.

"The thumbs, the thumbs, they hanged 'im by the thumbs…"

I was sure the message was aimed at me, even though I wasn't so innocent.

Halfway through the morning, an older white guy dropped a twenty-dollar tip. I hadn't seen too many twenties close up like that, so I wasn't sure at first if it was real. Diggy finished his song and took a break just then. Whether he noticed the double saw drop I didn't know, but he hollered for me to go buy him a pork chop sandwich at Jim's Original. Going by the way he yelled, I was sure he didn't like me anymore. I nodded at him and walked toward Jim's with the hat full of cash under my arm. When I turned the corner, I kept going, all the way to the El station.

I got off the train at Belmont and made my way over to Curiosity Corner, the novelty shop up on Broadway. The disguise kit I wanted cost seven bucks. It had different kinds of beards, mustaches, and sideburns. They looked real, nothing like the crummy Halloween kind. I paid for the kit, crossed the street to Woolworths, and bought a box of hair bleach like I'd seen a fugitive do in an old WGN movie. After that, I went to Amvets and picked out a second-hand suit, a button shirt, and a pair of wingtips like Ernie did when he was getting ready for court. I couldn't wait to get home and put my new look together.

Turning the corner onto our block, I saw a bunch of lumps out by the curb—furniture and other junk. As I got closer, I realized it was *our* furniture. I waited there excitedly, thinking Ernie was back and we were finally moving out of the projects, expecting him to walk out with an armful of stuff or pull a van around any second. He didn't. Inside the building, I stared at the red-lettered notice stuck to our door. Grown-up stuff like that always seemed like it was written in gibberish, but I knew my key wouldn't fit before I tried the lock.

I ran back to our measly possessions on the sidewalk. It looked like they'd been picked through already. I was pissed when I realized my boombox was gone. Then I got scared. I grabbed a few things—blankets, a cook pot, matches—and took them to "Issaquena", my spot by the river.

First thing I did when I got there was open the bleach and squeeze the goop onto my head. I had helped Loraine color her hair before, so I figured it couldn't be too hard. It was tingly at first, then it felt like the chemicals were really burning my scalp, so I ran to the river. The water smelled just like a hunk of meat left in the garbage too long, but I stuck my head in any way.

After that, I changed into my junk store clothes and fixed myself up with the disguise kit. I put on Diggy's hat too. It fit just right. With that whole getup on, I felt like a top-notch hobo, like Lee Marvin in *Emperor of the North*. When I walked back to the river's edge, I got spooked by my reflection. It was just like Ernie was there looking back at me.

It was colder than I thought it would be that night. I didn't get much sleep at all. In the morning, I went by Nino's to grab a cup of coffee and a donut. My old friend Carlos was coming out as I walked in. We'd been in the same basement class at Schneider. He was a "bilingual" because his family came from Mexico and didn't speak much English. I was a "learning disability" because I couldn't pay attention when teachers talked. Carlos's English got better. My attention didn't.

Carlos was wearing white clothes with paint all over them. He said he'd been working with his dad and uncles since school let out for summer. I asked him if it paid good. He said he could get me on the job if I wanted. I trailed him out to the van where his dad was waiting. They talked in Spanish a minute. I understood "pendejo" and "cabron." Carlos translated the rest.

"He say why you are wearing a fake mustache and having your hair in different colors."

When I pulled off the mustache, Carlos's dad shook his head and waved for me to get in.

We drove to a big frame house near Racine and Roscoe. I already knew my way around tools from helping Ernie wrench on cars. Carlos taught me how to call their names in Spanish so he wouldn't have to translate all the time. Some were fun to say, like *pinzas de perico* for channel locks and *llave de boca* for wrench.

The house was a big job. We were there more than a week. First, we scraped the wood and fixed it where pieces were missing. Then we caulked it here and there, coated it in white primer, and finally painted the whole place bright blue. The people coming in and out of the place had spiky hair and leather jackets with stuff written all over them. One of the girls from the house talked to me during lunch break on our last day there. She said her name was Ronnie and that she liked my "calico hair" and wingtips. I said I liked all her earrings, but what I really liked was how pretty she was and her big, round boobs. She invited me to come party at "Blue Hell"—the name they gave to their crash pad after we painted it. I couldn't wait for work to end so I could go talk to her.

When I knocked, Ronnie answered and introduced me around. There was a band living there called *Habitual Offense*. That made me think of Ernie. The singer had just moved out, so they were having band rehearsal without a singer while everyone sat around drinking beer and goofing off. I didn't like beer so much, but I had some anyway. When people were getting good and drunk, someone said,

"Hey, new guy, you sing?"

With all that beer in me, I nodded yes.

The bass player handed me a scrap of paper with words on it and pointed at a microphone. The drummer clicked his sticks together real fast, counting everybody in. They kept looking at me to do something, but I couldn't figure out when to sing. The third time they started, I closed my eyes and imagined I was Diggy out in the dirt lot by Maxwell Street. I started imitating his footstomps and head bobs and pretty soon I was singing too. But not the words on the paper, I was doing Whistlin' Shotgun instead.

When the band stopped playing, I opened my eyes. Ronnie was beaming at me. The other guys were smiling too.

"That was far out, man. You sounded like an old Black dude," the guitar player, John-O, said.

We did some more songs after that. I closed my eyes each time, picturing myself as Diggy, replacing their words with his. The guys argued about it awhile, but in the end, they decided I was in the band. John-O said we were the first punk group to ever have a blues singer. I was stoked to be called a blues singer and to be in a punk band.

Ronnie asked where I lived. I said "around." She pointed out the window and told me I could crash in the flat-tired van sitting in Blue Hell's driveway. It was getting late, and everyone was disappearing into their rooms so I took her up on it. It was a relief not going back to Issaquena.

Just after I fell asleep, Ronnie creaked open the van's rusty side door. She smelled like booze and cigarettes, like the way Loraine smelled when she insisted on kissing me good night. But I didn't mind with Ronnie. She climbed on top and wiggled off enough clothes so we could do it. When we were done fooling around, she played with my hair and said my lyrics were "so original," that they reminded her of the "beat poets." I didn't have the nerve to say they weren't my lyrics, and I didn't know about the beat poets. I never wanted her to stop playing with my hair.

That summer, I played two shows with *Habitual Offense*. One at Blue Hell, the other at an all-ages punk club called Space Place. The band wanted me to cut my hair and spike it like theirs. I wanted to leave it normal and wear Diggy's hat. The fedora helped me tap into Diggy's style but imitating him made me miss the real thing. Since I was afraid of going back to Maxwell Street, of facing him, I went to the downtown library and listened to his record instead. With the headphones cranked up, I could hear every string pop, every footstomp, and every worried bend in his voice. It felt like Diggy was right there with me.

I went back to the library at least once a week. The more I listened to Diggy's record, the closer I got to copping his feeling just right. But one day, when I showed up, the album was gone. I asked the librarian a lot of questions like who checked it out, when would it be back, and what if it didn't come back. She looked at me kind of stony and said it should be back in a week. So, I went back to the library the next week, and the next, but the record was always gone. I started losing hope of ever seeing it again. Funny thing, the longer I went without hearing Diggy, the worse my singing got. The band didn't say anything, but it seemed like they thought my voice was heading south too.

The last time I went to check on Diggy's album I decided to ask a librarian about Ronnie's beat poets. She showed me some books by Jack Kerouac and Allen Ginsberg and said I might like a Chicago writer named Nelson Algren too. The poetry didn't grab me, but Algren's stories did. He wrote about the kind of Chicago people I knew. Junkies, thieves, prostitutes, and street thugs. I read three stories from his book *The Neon Wilderness* before I left that day. When I walked outside, the world seemed more alive than it had before. Maybe more alive than ever.

Next time I went to the library, it was for books only. I even got a library card and started bringing some back to the van. It was funny, sitting in a busted van reading like that, like I was in my own little schoolhouse.

Ronnie invited me to spend the night in her room sometimes. I talked to her about the stories I was reading and how they reminded me of my own life. She said I should be a writer too. I didn't know what to write about. She said just write down the crazy stories I told her about Ernie and Loraine, so I started doing that.

The more I got into reading and writing, the less I wanted to sing with *Habitual Offense*. I skipped rehearsals whenever I could, but still gigged with them. We played the Cubby Bear, a sports bar across from Wrigley Field, that fall. There was a big crowd and we even got free beer. I left Diggy's hat off and spiked my hair, trying to look more punk like the guys wanted. My singing was lousy that night. No one said anything about it, but I was so embarrassed I quit after the show. I think the guys were relieved they didn't have to fire me. They found a new singer right away and did way better with him.

There was always a lot of drinking at Blue Hell, even more so when touring bands crashed there. One group, *Kooky and the Krackpots*, came all the way from California and stayed over for three nights in a row. I could tell Ronnie was ogling Kooky soon as they showed up. That landed me back in the broken van by myself. I knew Ronnie slept with other guys, but that time she acted like I didn't even exist. When The Krackpots finally split to play their next gig in Detroit, Ronnie left with them. Vince, the de facto leader of Blue Hell, said she wasn't coming back and asked if I wanted to rent her room. I was happy to move indoors with winter on the way, but it was sad sleeping in Ronnie's bed without her. It was so noisy in the house with all the partying and loud music, that I sometimes went back to the van anyway.

By the time spring came around, I was drinking as much as everyone else. The Blue Hellions were always looking for someone to pay for beer, and I was the only one with a job. I figured if I was paying, I might as well drink too. But the more I drank, the less I wanted to paint houses with Carlos. Little by little, I stopped showing up for work.

There was a girl named Sheila who started coming around the house. I didn't like her as much as Ronnie, but we fooled around once in a while. One day, when we were all totally wasted, a pair of clippers got passed around the living room. Sheila shaved my hair into a skinny mohawk, like hers, and pierced my left ear three times. The next day, she gave me a studded biker leather that she had found in our attic. Probably left by one of the touring bands. Sheila said it looked really sharp on me.

No one at Blue Hell was making money at that time, so we took turns panhandling. The thing was, begging reminded me too much of passing the hat for Diggy. Since I didn't want to spare change like everyone else, Vince appointed me "house chef," which meant I had to find ingredients too. John-O said I could dumpster-dive over by Jewel and A&P on certain days, but digging in the garbage was gross, so I hit up food pantries instead.

When the churches near Blue Hell got sick of me coming around, I had to go farther and farther out in search of grub. One day, I went clear over to Buena Presbyterian in Uptown to hit up a pantry. It was a good score. I walked out of there with an army backpack full of rice, dry beans, cans of pork, and a giant block of government cheese. As I started hoofing it back toward the house, I heard someone shout, "Hey, kid!"

My whole body tightened. I walked faster, hoping he'd think it was mistaken identity. But I could hear his shoes. Slapping the sidewalk hard and fast. That horrible sound when you know someone is coming for you and there's nothing you can do to get away.

"Thought you'd duck the ol' man with that getup?" He said, sidling up next to me.

For the first time in my life, I didn't want Ernie to be out of jail. I didn't want him to call me kid, or do his stupid laugh, or follow me back to Blue Hell and rip everyone off. I didn't want him to be my real-life, fucked up dad. I wanted him to stay put under a stained mattress in a broken van where what he did and said was confined to the straight lines of a spiral notebook's ruled paper.

Ernie talked fast, telling me that he only pulled a year on the burglary beef, and that his Narcotics Anonymous sponsor, Lenny, got him a job pushing broom at a college, and that he was staying at the Wilson Men's Hotel temporarily, and that his life was "back on track." I stopped listening after that.

Flagging down a southbound bus, I said I'd come by sometime, hurrying off without looking at his eyes. I didn't have to see them to know they were pinned, that he was high as a kite.

He hollered after me, "You should find a better disguise next time!"

I thought, *next time, you should too.*

8.

C'ree

Meg and James Flanagan were professors at the University of Cincinnati where James ran the chamber music program at the College-Conservatory of Music and Meg was an associate professor in the English Department. Neither had wanted to become a career academic, but when Meg became pregnant during her and James' respective Bachelor programs, they had to make hard choices. James went on to pursue a Masters in music, deciding that the teaching path, rather than performance, would be the safest bet. Meg also gave up creative endeavors, leaving a half-written novel behind to tend to students and her baby girl, Carrie.

At age five, Carrie's exacting father began training her in the living room of their large Victorian-era home, having her practice violin no less than three hours a day. Mother Meg, also expecting a high-achieving child, had Carrie reading Homer's Odyssey at age six. Under her parents' tutelage, young Carrie gained admittance to the best schools and programs Cincinnati had to offer. All went well for a time, but by third grade Carrie had entered a new phase of development. Through small acts of rebellion—spilling fruit juice on homework, losing her backpack, breaking her violin bow—Carrie began to show signs that she wasn't interested in following the path of Meg and James.

At ten years old, after dipping into cocktail dregs at a grown-up party, Carrie began exploring the marvels of her parent's liquor cabinet. At first it was a game. She and her friends would take sips of this one and that one to see who could remain standing the longest. But Carrie soon ran out of friends who were interested in the sport, who could keep up with her, or who were even allowed to visit the Flanagan home.

At thirteen, having skipped a grade the previous year, Carrie entered high school. Happily, she met children there who shared her enjoyment of drinking, and who, like her, could remain standing after many sips of this one and that one. Through those kinships, Carrie was introduced to other mood-altering substances of which she soon became quite fond. As such, schoolwork sank to the bottom of her priority list.

Toward the end of Carrie's sophomore year, her new boyfriend—a twenty-year-old rock guitarist named Del—snuck her into a downtown Cincinnati dive bar to see renowned r&b singer H-Bomb Ferguson. H-Bomb, an elderly, skeletally thin Black man who wore a blonde bangs-and-bob Doris Day wig, pounded piano keys to the brink of breaking while a police gumball attached at the instrument's top whirred red light around the room. The well-worn one-liners H-Bomb delivered between raunchy blues and boogie-woogies made Carrie, Del, and the entire bar crowd convulse with laughter—not so much for the jokes themselves, but for the bluesman's idiosyncratic way of wisecracking. The first time Carrie saw H-Bomb was the last time she played violin.

The following year, Del moved from his parents' home in Northern Kentucky into a rundown tenement flat shared by his bandmates in Cincinnati's Over-the-Rhine neighborhood. The band, a retro psychedelic-rock group called *Over-the-Rhine Bozos* whose logo was Judy Garland as Dorothy bent over a rainbow getting boinked from behind by Bozo the Clown, were well known in the Cincy scene for their heavy drinking and drug use. None more so than Del, who had landed in his new digs, "the OTRB house," after his parents became fed up with finding syringes and blackened spoons littering their home.

Carrie's high school was less than a half mile from the OTRB house, from Del, affording her more interesting and accessible opportunities for class-ditching than she'd had in previous years. Setting aside school to receive a more enticing education from Del and his guitar, Carrie, with her well-established musical discipline, soon equaled him on the instrument. And with Del's musical abilities decreasing as his heroin use increased, it wasn't long before Carrie was the superior player.

Ever up for an adventure, Carrie let it be known she wanted a go at the nefarious narcotic Del put his attentions toward. Though he feigned a protective stance on the matter, Del's half-hearted attempts to discourage her from dope use were short-lived. The first time Carrie dipped into Del's bag, she vomited all over the OTRB couch, which left her unclear as to whether she liked the drug or not. But recalling the fondness she'd found for tequila after a similar, initial encounter, she tried Del's drugs again. And again. And again.

Soon, she began accompanying Del on his drug runs. Carrie would wait in the van—and later, after he sold the van, would wait on the sidewalk—while he slinked inside a dopehouse to do the deals. But as Del spent an ever-increasing interval in the dealer's den—hunting a viable vein or blowing the bag-holder, she imagined—bringing an ever-decreasing share back for Carrie, she tired of the routine and demanded to go in with him.

"Is that name for real? Maybe we should start calling you *Dante*," Carrie laughed at meeting Del's dealer, Virgil.

But unlike her, Del hadn't read The Divine Comedy, the first book forced by Mother Meg that Carrie had felt a kinship with. The cerebral quip, like so many of Carrie's cracks, sailed over Del's doped-out skull and dissolved, unfulfilled, into the space behind him.

By the start of senior year, Carrie was visiting Virgil unaccompanied, entering her own exploration of the inferno's agonizing rings. But dabbling in the addictive drug didn't seem a problem to seventeen-year-old Carrie Flanagan, who only "partied" on heroin once or twice or three times a month. Dope addiction struck her as a lifestyle choice. Del, she was certain, had taken on the role of junkie to become more like his hero, Keith Richards. But unlike the rock god he worshipped, Del was neither rich nor famous, and had no support network to help him as heroin began to take its toll.

After pawning his Les Paul one dopesick morning, and subsequently ripping off everyone at the OTRB house, it became clear to all who knew him that the thieving, beady-eyed skeleton who they still referred to as Del—though he now bared little resemblance to the man they'd once known—had been fully absorbed into the desolate, musicless void of drug dependency.

Carrie, on the other hand, was more excited about music than ever. The day Del got booted from the OTRB house, she went home and dug her dusty violin out from under the bed. Selling the upscale instrument to a collector, she searched out a suitable replacement for practicing her new musical passion: pre-war era blues. Excitedly, she spotted a 1930s-era Regal arch-top in the window of a downtown pawnshop and knew it was destined to be hers. As she paid the pawnbroker for the antique acoustic, Carrie caught sight of an Over-the-Rhine Bozos logo emblazoned on the back of a cherry-red Gibson dangling behind the counter.

"*Just two guitars passing in a pawnshop,*" she waxed, knowing it was over between them.

Attending class just enough to keep from failing, Carrie spent the majority of her school hours seeking out country blues recordings by masters like Skip James, Blind Boy Fuller, and Mississippi Fred McDowell. At home, in her bedroom, she imitated the intricate fingerpickings and soulful moans of the musicians she obsessed over. Wishing she was from another time, another place, and most of all, another race. Though her parents were relieved she had broken up with Del, they were irritated by the endless clamor of unrefined music emanating from her room.

Ditching biology class one day, Carrie discovered a promising-looking album in a cutout bin at Rory's Records. Rory, who was usually knowledgeable about lesser-known musical figures, had little insight to offer Carrie when she brought the album, *People's Always Dyin'* by Diggy Nubbit, up to the cash register. After reading the liner notes, Rory rang up the record and said, "Says he plays on Maxwell Street. That's the real Chicago deal, right there."

In her room, dropping the needle on Diggy's disc, Carrie's pulse fluttered, following the unusual rhythm of side A, track one, "Whistlin' Shotgun." Sitting transfixed before the stereo, drawn in by the rawness of guitar, vocals, and footstomps crackling through her speakers, Carrie's baseline sadness, the ever-present weight that had informed her every action since childhood, began to grow new limbs—tentacles that reached through speakers, through songs, through time itself. It seemed that Diggy's strange, heavy-hearted ballads were not recordings at all, but dormant parts of her own being, now awakening through blood, lymph, and bone, becoming known at long last. Weeping and writhing in her bed until sunup, Carrie played the album on repeat, knowing the next stop on her musical journey would be Maxwell Street.

On the seven-hour Greyhound ride to Chicago the next day, Carrie considered the differences between Diggy's record and other blues records she'd enjoyed. Though she searched her mind for stylistic comparisons, she could think of no other musician, no matter how expressive, who was remotely similar to Diggy Nubbit. Shining his dark light on her soul, Diggy made every other singer seem detached, shallow, performative. Though Carrie, like parents Meg and James, had never considered herself a spiritual person, the discovery of Diggy Nubbit made her suddenly curious about such things.

After the long trip, it was exciting to arrive at the dirty, sprawling bazaar known as Maxwell Street Market. Wading through throngs of sellers, shoppers, singers, and day drunks, Carrie kept her eyes and ears peeled for Diggy. After an hour of combing the market, a mournful moan that seemed to emanate from all four directions at once hit her in the head and chest. Turning down alleys and up side streets, Carrie searched frantically for its origin. Finally, in a small dirt lot at the edge of Maxwell Street, between a dented bathtub and a three-wheeled grocery cart loaded with broken bricks, she found him. Sitting atop two stacked milk crates, his grey hair sticking out in tufts from beneath a faded brown fedora, Diggy plucked notes out of his five-stringed guitar with the intensity of a mother removing lice from a child's head, flicking the music into space as if banishing it from his instrument. The spectacle dropped Carrie to her knees.

The emotional turmoil that had enveloped Carrie while listening to Diggy at home was tenfold in the presence of the blues master. But more than her inner world, it was the sudden changes around her, the rapid movements of sights and sounds, that made her head spin. For as Diggy picked, moaned, stomped, and groaned, the outer world—the entire animate and inanimate environment of the shabby backlot, from ground to sky—transformed into a shimmering puppet show of luminosity, an ominous swirling force that left Carrie without a single reference point from her young life to draw upon. In a desperate attempt to ground herself, Carrie pulled her arch-top from its case and began accompanying the bluesman as best she could. The bright smile that lit up Diggy's face in that moment let Carrie know she was exactly where she was meant to be.

After graduating high school, though just barely, Carrie spent her weekends in Chicago, taking it upon herself to look after her new mentor, Diggy. In turn, the bluesman shared the secrets of his tunings and tempos, phrasings and philosophies, as well as the twists and turns of his unusual life with the "white gal from Sinchanatty" who he called "C'ree."

Cleaning his apartment and helping him get around town were simple enough tasks. But providing for Diggy proved difficult as his only income was a meager once-a-month government check, and Carrie's only cash was whatever she could pilfer from her father's wallet. Hoping to generate more funds, she began seeking out gigs for Diggy in Black-owned blues clubs on Chicago's West and South Sides. Offering promotional cassette copies of Diggy's LP, *Peoples Always Dyin'*, Carrie soon found that Black club owners and patrons knew exactly who Diggy Nubbit was, that they did not need to hear the tape. Not only did they not need to hear it, they refused to let her leave a copy on their premises. And not only did they not let her leave a copy, they pointed the way out the moment she evoked his name. In those circles, Black circles, Carrie soon discovered, Diggy was known as a singing sorcerer, a walking, talking talisman of trouble.

When the Black clubs didn't work out, Carrie moved on to the white-populated venues of Chicago's North Side where fewer people had a take on Diggy. The farther north—and further away from Maxwell Street—she went, the more luck she had securing shows for her mentor. Through her persuasive charm, Carrie easily booked paying gigs for Diggy at three separate locations: a folkie coffee shop, a Ukrainian restaurant, and a neighborhood sports bar.

Diggy's North Side tour, however, was to be short-lived. By the time he'd played his second show, word had gotten around of "clear-the-room-Nubbit"—a handy act to have at one time of the night only: closing time. In the end, no one invited the bizarro blues bard to jinx their joint more than once. The remote backlot he'd occupied every Sunday for over thirty years remained Diggy's only performance opportunity.

Anyone but Carrie might have wondered why the bad luck bluesman bothered performing each Sunday on Maxwell Street given the lack of audience and financial incentive. But she knew. Diggy *had* to play. It was a force he couldn't control. A power he had to honor and obey. Carrie envisioned him as the keeper of a cosmic darkness. A darkness she believed Diggy must tend to, not for himself, but for all of humanity. She knew, as Diggy did, that the darkness he voiced belonged to everyone, that it was always there waiting for them. A beautiful darkness that had the power to transform… if they would just let it in.

When Carrie considered the problem, she could see it wasn't any one thing about Diggy that bothered people so much. Not just his thousand-yard stare, or the peculiarity of his voice, or his bizarre lyrics, or his unusual guitar style. Any one of those things on their own wasn't so terribly off-putting. But expressed all at once, along with the off-kilter timing of his left foot pounding the hard Chicago earth, they became extremely triggering. It never took more than a few bars of song for the effects to kick in. She'd seen it again and again. Whatever anxieties, worst fears, and hidden traumas one held in the depths of their body, Diggy, like a Pied-Piper of pain, brought bubbling to the surface. To Carrie this was the real reason he was called Diggy. For his ability to dig up people's wounds, leaving them in a terrifying state of uncertainty about who, what, and where they were. Like everyone who encountered Diggy and his mournful melodies, Carrie spent nearly every moment with him in that vulnerable state. Every moment, that is, when she wasn't shooting dope.

As Carrie frequented Diggy's place, a two-room flat in the rat and roach-infested Patrick Sullivan Senior Apartments at the corner of Madison and Ashland, she spent an ever-increasing amount of time in his bathroom. But the dope she copped in the projects, just one floor below Diggy's digs, was stronger than the stuff she scored in Cincinnati. As such, Carrie soon moved on from once, twice, or three times a month. It wasn't a party anymore. When Mother Meg found a needle in Carrie's closet on one of her hunting expeditions, she paraded it around the house, yelling about ingratitude and the waste of a wonderful education. With the problems at home, Carrie left Cincy for good.

A few days after moving to Chicago, Carrie landed a waitressing job at Peter's Broasted Chicken near Fullerton and Halsted. Her diner gig afforded her a small apartment—just a short bus ride from her mentor's place—with enough cash left over to take the edge off when she needed to.

Nearly all of Carrie's non-working hours were spent with Diggy, and the more time she spent with him, the more Diggy-like she became. Though she diligently imitated his dialect, guitar fingerings, and odd sense of timing, there was something much stronger at play in Carrie's transformation. Diggy had opened a door and Carrie had stepped through. The emotional entrainment that transpired within that otherworldly space caused two heartbeats to become one.

On Sundays, during Diggy's breaks in the dirt lot, Carrie took the singer's seat—the two-high-stacked, faded orange milk crates. And when she picked and groaned his songs, passersby were repelled by her performance nearly as much as if it were the old man himself.

"Ain't nobody want to hear the truth," Diggy reminded her when she bemoaned the people's aversion.

From then on, Carrie, like Diggy, no longer had a choice when it came to singing out that terrible truth. But in her case, giving voice to the volatile vibrations required an ever-heftier dose of H. As such, daily visits to see her latest Virgil on the West Side became choiceless, too. Between the heroin and the emotional toll of "hole-digging," Carrie's eyes drooped to near-shut—dimming the formerly bright backlot to a faint glow—as she belted out Diggy ditties Sunday after Sunday.

And so it was that on one of those Sundays, a quirky boy sitting before her in the dirt, mouthing along to every syllable, went completely undetected by Carrie.

It wasn't until she heard Diggy shout, "Hey now, Steve! Where you been bwah?" that she noticed the punky-looking kid, smiling sheepishly up at the bluesman.

The softness in the boy's face set against the darkness of the hole-digging was shocking to Carrie. Even stranger was the fact that he, too, seemed to share a bond with Diggy. As she listened to the joy in their voices, Carrie felt a lightness in herself she hadn't experienced in months.

At the end of the afternoon, as Diggy packed his guitar and took the bus back to the projects, Carrie and Steve walked through the market discussing Diggy's music and what it meant to each of them. Her rendition of "Whistlin' Shotgun," Steve said, was the best he'd ever heard. When she found out he was living in an abandoned van outside a punk flophouse, she invited him to her place.

Within a few days, Steve became too hard to deal with at couch distance. He was more wounded than Del or anyone else Carrie had been with. It felt good to touch him and even better to take care of him. The time they spent together—her teaching Steve guitar, him sharing stories about his life—even helped her stay off stuff. Steve dreamt out loud about the two of them traveling the world, playing the blues, writing stories about it all. Carrie smiled along with the fantasy, but she knew good and well that the darkness she carried, the hole-digging, couldn't be shared beyond Diggy's Maxwell Street lot.

Two months after Steve moved in, there were signs she was carrying something else as well. With Del and other men, condoms had always been part of it, but the boy, she had assumed, was too innocent, too much a child himself to produce a child. It was just play, not real, grown-up sex. After two at-home tests, she finally faced facts.

With one tough-luck kid in her bed, another in her belly, and Diggy's darkness suffusing every cell of her being, depression added more weight to Carrie's body than her feet could support. She called in sick to Peter's one morning and lay on the bedroom floor, staring at cracks in the ceiling. That night, when Steve came home from painting houses, she asked him to look too. When he didn't see what she saw, Carrie was relieved, but the images kept coming, cracking through her thoughts and dreams.

The next day, Carrie didn't bother calling in to work. Her lower belly, as if filled with a rapidly growing lead weight, had become so dense that cracks formed in the ground below her as well. When Steve left for work that morning, she clawed tightly to the floor. But it was no use. Nine circles below, Virgil was waiting, ready to punch twenty-dollar holes in her upper-world problems.

When Carrie came home that evening, Steve recognized the pinpointed pupils but didn't mention it. He didn't say anything at all until they were in bed, staring at the ceiling.

"I see them now," he said, pointing at the cracks above.

In the morning, when Steve found out she was going to Cincinnati, he begged to go with. It seemed like a bad idea, but Carrie relented, knowing her parents would be away that weekend. Downtown at the Randolph Street station, Carrie cooked two twenties in the bathroom, saving a little for later. For the duration of the Greyhound ride, Steve held her hand. Not out of affection, but to make sure his nodding girlfriend still had a pulse.

When they arrived, Carrie found the key under a planter full of dead flowers and let them in. Steve was amazed by the giant home that had as many books as a library. He stayed in the living room reading while Carrie loaded a few of her parents' more valuable possessions into a backpack, saying she'd be back soon.

The couple were fast asleep when Carrie's parents came home from their trip. Meg followed the trail of clothes and White Castle boxes to Carrie's former bedroom. Finding her track-marked daughter in the sack with a naked boy, she made a face of disgust—one she wished someone would've witnessed—and slammed the door hard to make her opinion better known. James, ignoring the commotion, went upstairs to practice Brahms on the viola.

After the door slam, which caused the lovers to bolt up in bed, Carrie sighed and lumbered out to the living room, where her mother was pouring a drink. Meg, ever ready with mixed-up literary references, said, "Let me guess, a young prince broke the spell of your *magical negro*."

"I need money, Meg."

"Are you asking me to buy the drugs or hire a lawyer for your jailbait problem?"

"I need an abortion."

Carrie watched as the tumbler of bourbon slipped from Meg's hand and smashed on the polished wood floor. It was the hole-digging. Same as singing a Diggy song.

After a moment of deafening silence, Meg yelled, "I'll give you the money. I wouldn't want you to go through life with as much disappointment in your child as I have in *you*!"

On the bus back to Chicago, Steve stared quietly at cornfields and billboards. Carrie, with dopesickness already churning her blood and bones, tried making conversation to take her mind off things. Knowing it was almost Steve's birthday, she asked how it felt to be turning seventeen.

"Actually, I'm only fifteen tomorrow," he said awkwardly, unable to lie any longer.

"I know," Carrie said.

When he fell asleep on the bus, Carrie wrote a note on the cash-stuffed envelope Meg had reluctantly given her:

Dear Steve,

You are the most curious person I've ever met, which is another way of saying I love you more than anyone. These months with you have been the happiest of my life. No one has ever done anything good for you and that breaks my heart. The only good thing I can do is stop seeing you. It doesn't sound like a birthday present, but believe me it is. The problems I have will only hurt you more. Please don't look for me. When you see Diggy tell him I love him too. Maybe someday you'll write a story for me?

Yours always,
C'ree

When they arrived at the Randolph Street terminal, Carrie asked if he wanted to see a movie. Steve pointed at the marquee down the block. It was almost showtime when they walked in.

As the lights dimmed in the seedy, formerly ornate space of The Oriental, they fell into a depressive calm. Carrie tucked the note into their popcorn bucket and whispered that she was going to the bathroom. While kids jumped around the front row, imitating Bruce Lee's dexterous moves, Steve fingertraced initials carved in the wooden armrest of his seat, saying to no one in particular that he'd seen this one before.

9.

Obituary Writer

I popped my quarters in a Sun-Times box and snatched out two copies. That was the Ernie in me. Every year since he went away, it got a little better, but taking more than my share still came as natural as breathing. At Chester's, I ordered coffee and a bowl of rice and gravy, leaving the extra paper on the counter to atone for my Ernie-ness. I rarely looked at a paper, unless there was nothing else to read, but that day, June 3rd, 1990, I read every word on every page. I needed to take my time getting to Diggy's obituary.

I already knew what it would say since I wrote it, but I wanted to see it in print. A sense of finality maybe, or vanity. I'd never seen my words published before. In either case, I hoped, wherever she was, Carrie would see it too. It was the Sunday paper, so it took me a while getting there. News, op-eds, sports, and entertainment all went in one eyeball and out the other. Nothing landed but the three cups of coffee I downed on my way to the obits. Carrie used to say I used coffee to "self-medicate" depression. I'll admit I liked coffee about as much as she liked dope, but I never heard of anyone dying from a coffee O.D.

The actor Rex Harrison from Dr. Dolittle had died the same day as Diggy. *Sir Reginald "Rex" Harrison, A Leading Man with Urbane Wit, Dies at 82,* the headline said. There must've been a half-page on him. As I read about Rex, I thought about the five short paragraphs I had put together on Diggy. Some of the info was regurgitated from the liner notes on back of his only recorded album, but most came from little things he'd disclosed to me over the years, like his belief in the healing power of petunias, his ability to teach a cockroach to sing, and the fact that he had only one testicle. I didn't mention that his brutal father had beaten the nut off him with a switch. That seemed too gory for the general public.

When I reached the bottom of the obituary section, I found a heavily redacted version of the piece I had sent in. I flipped the page, thinking it might continue, but it didn't. There was no headline. No photo. Nothing there about how Diggy got his nickname from working as a gravedigger his whole life, or how his music was too sad (even for the blues), or how he let a fifteen-year-old white boy named Steve Bardo live with him in the Patrick Sullivan senior projects at Madison and Ashland for the entire winter of 1983. All that remained were a few simple facts: *Alonzo "Diggy" Nubbit, Delta bluesman who performed regularly at the Maxwell Street Market, dies at 75.* I was surprised to read, though, that there would be a memorial service that afternoon at A.A. Rayner and Sons Funeral Home. I couldn't imagine who would've put that together.

Needing to cleanse my palate after the stunted obit, I ordered more coffee and moved on to the classifieds. Though I hadn't planned on doing so, I began searching for a new job. Anything was better than the box fan factory where I'd been working for the past six months.

Assembly line, Bartender, Delivery, Demolition laborer, Experienced obituary writer...

I got excited by the last one, figuring, at least technically, I did have experience. I ripped the ad from the paper and went to the toilet, letting a quart of coffee go from my bladder. When I checked the big industrial clock on the diner's back wall, I saw it was just two hours until Diggy's memorial.

I stopped at my place and changed into a junk store blazer and a pair of wingtips before taking the El to the South Side. When I arrived at A.A. Rayner and Sons, I walked into the vestibule and stood snacking on a bowl of caramels set out on an end table, waiting politely for someone to escort me in. Ten minutes later, and still no sign of life, I entered the main room. But there was no one there either. No greeter, no music, not even any chairs set up. I found Diggy, though. He was in a corner, laid out in an open casket, his face covered in pancake makeup like a silent film actor. I imagined him suddenly opening his eyes and flapping his lips to the tinkle of a player piano, communicating via subtitles that rolled on the bottom of the box.

"May I help you?" came a soft voice from behind.

I turned and saw an attractive, well-dressed young Black woman.

"I'm a friend of Diggy's."

"A friend of whom?"

"The deceased. Am I early for the service?"

"This is the correct time. There just haven't been many visitors yet."

"There were other visitors?"

"Actually, no. You're the first."

When she saw the confusion on my face, she continued.

"I'm afraid we weren't given much direction by Mr. Nubbit's former employers. As to making a program or offering other amenities."

"You mean the *cemetery*? Are they paying for this?" I asked.

"Yes, that's right. I was told Mr. Nubbit worked at Oak Woods for quite a long time. They've chosen to honor his years of service with a memorial and burial plot."

It seemed weird to call it a memorial when there were only two of us there and nothing to inspire memories other than a creepily-painted dead man in a cheap box, which, if anything, brought on memories of low-budget horror movies. Still, it was comforting to be in the lady's presence. Her face was round and her light black skin was smooth. Her lips, like two fluffy pillows, were so inviting, I couldn't help but let my gaze rest on them, though probably a bit too long. I've been told I do that. Carrie used to say it anyway. Feeling self-conscious for staring, I started rambling on about Diggy. Before I got too far, a tall Black guy wearing a bowtie stepped in and said, "We shall now move on from calling hours and begin our procession to Oak Woods."

The pretty woman handed me an orange sticker with the word *FUNERAL* on it.

"You may follow the hearse to Oak Woods if you plan to attend the burial," she said.

I didn't have the nerve to tell her I was on foot.

"Thanks so much, Miss…?"

"Shirley Goodrich," she said, extending both hands for a warm handshake.

I walked a mile and a half to the cemetery, holding the funeral sticker in front of me like a shield, hoping it would help if I was accosted for being the lone white guy in an all-Black neighborhood. It's a fact that I'd often been the lone white guy when I visited Diggy, but it was different now. For one thing, the main thing, he was dead. I had no living friend in this corner of Chicago.

When I finally arrived at the massive graveyard, it took some time to find Diggy's plot. Two Oak Woods' employees—Latino men in their thirties or so—were lowering him into the ground just as I walked up. They looked too young to have known Diggy. I asked anyway.

"Dibby Nuggets? Never heard of it," one of them said, as the casket hit the earth.

There was no ceremony.

Though I left the cemetery vowing never to forget the great bluesman, I mostly thought about Shirley Goodrich on the northbound El ride home. Sitting on the train, chomping A.A. Raynor's caramels, I pulled the classified clipping from my wallet. Writing obituaries, I figured, would put me in the same general field of work as Shirley.

The next morning, I gathered my short story notebooks—to prove I was a writer—and went to apply for the obituary job. When I entered the office of The Avondale Gazette, a small brick storefront near Belmont and Milwaukee, I found two people working busily in a narrow room—an old woman wearing an out-of-date wig on one side and a middle-aged man at a typewriter on the other.

"I'm here for the job," I said.

The two lifted their heads simultaneously, gave me the once-over, and quickly returned to whatever they were doing. Without eyeballing me again, the woman reached her big knuckles toward a door at the back of the room and rapped hard. A bald man in his seventies came out, splashing coffee out of a mug as he did so.

"Who are you?" he asked.

"Steve Bardo... obituary writer," I said, as confidently as possible.

"Mówisz po polsku?"

I shook my head.

"Spanish?"

"Poquito," I said.

"We print in three languages for seven neighborhoods," the old man barked.

The cheap wig woman, now on the phone, covered the mouthpiece and rasped, "Everything's translated by the other office, and you know it, Aloysius."

"But the kid's gotta make his calls," the old man countered.

"It isn't 1947. People speak English at funeral homes, Al," she said.

"The job pays shit," typewriter guy interjected, without looking up.

"Give him the sheet, see how he does," Al said, spilling more coffee and disappearing into the back room.

The woman, who introduced herself as Dolores, sighed,

"Here's the sheet. Find out who kicked the bucket, who's left, and where the party is. Keep the bios short and sweet." Then, waving a long, bony finger at my t-shirt and jeans added, "Show up tomorrow in slacks and a button shirt. Al doesn't like casual *attire*."

In the most cluttered area of the office, directly adjacent the bathroom, I began unburdening the sole unoccupied desk of fake plants, hardened jars of rubber cement, and broken staplers. The chair, which I reluctantly sat on, was four inches too short for the desk, as if a person with incredibly short legs and long torso had once manned that particularly sad station. Slightly disappointed at getting the job so easily, I stuffed my notebooks in a drawer and picked up "the sheet"—a barely legible laminated page that looked like it was from 1947. When I glanced back at Dolores, she was staring in my direction, making a dialing motion in the air with her right pointer finger and a pinky-thumb phone with her left. I waited a minute, imagining she might do other feats, like trapped-in-a-box or walking-in-the-wind, but when I didn't immediately follow her pantomimed instructions, she only wrinkled her already deeply wrinkled brow and snuffed at me.

As I started calling around, it became clear many of the numbers listed on the sheet—twelve funeral parlors, twenty-one old folks' homes, and the Cook County morgue—had been changed or were no longer in service. When someone did pick up, I introduced myself as "Steve Bardo, obituary writer for The Avondale Gazette." But gathering information was difficult. The people on the other end either didn't want to be bothered or else cracked bizarre jokes about their recent dead.

An hour later, reviewing my notes, I wondered how to keep the five obituaries I'd been tasked with writing from sounding the same. I searched the desk, hoping to find an 'obituary template' or something, but there were no instructions, nothing to show how to do it. Before I could give it another thought, my phone rang. It was Dolores. She was less than ten feet away, so it was a little awkward, but I went along with it just the same.

"Turn it over," she rasped, like a film noir femme fatale.

With the phone cradled at my ear, I flipped the sheet over and found a numbered list of tasks: 1. Clean entire office (toilet!). 2. Sweep/shovel sidewalk. 3. Maintain Xerox. 4. "Miscellaneous" errands. 5. DO NOT MAKE COFFEE (Dolores only).

"Okay," I said.

"Start by emptying the waste baskets, then come get this package from my desk," she ordered.

After dropping Dolores's package at the post office, I decided to take an early lunch. At a nearby diner called Bobak's, I ate a bowl of borscht while studying a Chicago Tribune left on the counter, memorizing death notice jargon like: "departed her earthly body," "ended a long battle with," and "the bereaved will gather." None of the obituaries offered any genuine insight into a person, the actual ups and downs of their lives. It was depressing.

After an hour of one-one-thousanding along with the greasy clock behind the grill, contemplating whether or not to go back to the office, I ordered a fifth cup of coffee. The waitress, rather than returning with the carafe, slid a check under my cup with a tightness of lip that suggested I had surpassed Bobak's refill point. Equally tight of lip, I flipped the check over and began scribbling out an obituary for the time I had killed sitting at her counter—more of an assisted suicide than murder, I decided—and left it by the register along with my last three dollars.

After a long, boring battle with seconds, Mr. Fifty-nine Longhand Minutes passed away peacefully at Bobak's "Not-So-Bottomless-Cup" Restaurant. The deceased is survived by his grieving widow Mrs. Shorthand Minutes (née Hours) and their four children, Day, Week, Month, and Year. The bereaved will gather below the industrial wall clock at The Avondale Gazette.

"I don't have a typewriter," I announced when I got back.

Dolores frowned and pointed toward the basement door. I felt disappointed that she didn't mime walking-down-stairs or call me on the desk phone to whisper secret instructions. Opening the basement door, I was overcome with a heavy waft of mold. The frayed string that switched on the basement's lone, bare bulb snapped as I yanked it—an obvious metaphor for the decline of my mental faculties since taking a job at The Avondale Gazette. There, in the semi-dark, sifting through mounds of broken things, I found a couple of ancient typing machines that were clearly not meant for modern fingers. When I reemerged empty-handed, the middle-aged man, who rarely took a break from typing, snatched a key off a corkboard and unlocked a closet full of office supplies. After handing me a modern-ish electric typewriter, he introduced himself as Herb and went back to clacking noisily on his own machine. An hour later, he squeaked his wheely chair behind me and peered over my shoulder.

"A-S-D-F J-K-L-semi-colon," he said, addressing my single-finger typing technique. "Your grammar's shit," he added, opening a file cabinet and tossing a massive book called *The Manual of Style* in front of me.

Not wanting to seem ungrateful, I pretend-read the book for several minutes.

At the end of the day, I took the five obituaries I had typed and offered them to Dolores, who I assumed was in charge of things.

"Less you're bringing coffee'n Danish, don't drop nothing on my desk," she said, dismissively.

Without taking his eyes off the page in front of him, Herb waved me over. He thumbed through my obits for all of five seconds and then shot me a sideways glance.

"Done any writing before, kid?" He asked.

I smiled and pulled the notebooks from my desk.

My first weeks at The Avondale Gazette were a struggle. The obituaries I wrote so painstakingly had to be edited by Herb each time. He wasn't happy with the extra work, but after reading my short stories, he warmed up a bit. Herb said I should consider typing them up and sending them around. He especially liked the one I had written about a thief's soul getting trapped in a stolen object—a story based loosely on letters Ernie had sent from Menard penitentiary over his, by then, eight years of incarceration. I didn't tell Herb the thief was my dad. *Less people know about you, the better*, I thought. Another Ernie-ism.

With Diggy dead, and Ernie locked up, Herb became something of a father figure. Besides sharing his favorite authors and giving pointers on writing, he taught me how to roll cigarettes—a French brand called Gauloises that you could only get from a tobacconist in the South Loop. I also began imitating his scholarly lingo, using words like *ephemeral*, *diminutive*, and *pernicious*.

Herb brought the topic of romance into our conversation quite a bit. He said it was important for writers not to become "perniciously isolated." I could tell he wanted me to divulge my love life, as he often did, but it was too embarrassing to admit that my sole romantic interest was a lady I had met only briefly at a memorial service for a dead man that no one cared about but me. Herb was pretty smart, though. He noticed how possessive I was of the bright orange "bookmark" that was ever dangling from one novel or another on my desk. But the feelings wrapped up in that funeral sticker—about Shirley, about Diggy—were too much to explain, even to myself.

As Herb continually pitted romance against isolation, my relationship fantasy about Shirley heightened. Worrying that the ephemeral window of opportunity I had with her—diminutive as it was—might fade completely, I added A.A. Rayner and Sons Funeral Home to my sheet and began calling there during my daily rounds. I braced myself every time, but it was always a machine with a man's voice. Bowtie guy, I figured. Finally, one late September afternoon, after calling four times in a row, a woman picked up. I started talking. Fast.

"Hello, this is Steve Bardo. Obituary writer for *The Sun-Times*. I'm calling to see if you have anyone for us?"

In a professional tone, the woman gave details about a service they would host that weekend. I interrupted.

"Is this Shirley Goodrich by any chance?"

"Do I know you?"

"Diggy Nubbit's memorial. You gave me a funeral sticker…"

"White boy with the old-timey suit? You work for the Sun-Times?"

I felt bad about lying, but it was too late.

"I write for various papers… in three languages. But I recognized your voice right away."

That last bit seemed to charm her. I was about to tell her that I still had the funeral sticker, that I was reminded of her every time I saw it, but that seemed too over-the-top. Trying to sound impressive, I mentioned that I was actually a fiction writer, short stories, and that I only did obituaries for money.

"Obituaries pay better than fiction?" she asked.

It hadn't occurred to me that my stories might pay something. Drawing a blank, I excused myself and got off the phone. Herb was staring at me when I hung up. I turned away and resumed work before he could say anything. With my mind still on Shirley, I went down the sheet, ringing up contacts, collecting the usual obit info. On my last call, I got an earful from a guy named Arnie, the gossipiest mortician in my network.

"Check this out. Got a twenty-two-year-old Mexican on the slab. Girlfriend did it. Story is, she answers a call meant for him...from a *VD clinic*. Nurse tells her that boyfriend is negative for syphilis or whatever. But now, girlfriend knows he's cheating, right? So, get this, she runs him over at the carwash... *where he works.*"

When he was done with the dramatic punchline, Arnie gave me more pertinent details, including the fact that the dead man's family would be coming up from Chihuahua, Mexico for the service. I typed up two versions of the obituary, as I sometimes did, turning in the print version to Herb at the end of the day. My "sideline obit," a stylized rendition that I would've normally stashed in a desk drawer along with other creative writing, must've been left in the typewriter.

From Autumn to Afterlife

Just as leaves let go of the tree,
José has released himself from the earthly realm.
He departed this world from his place of employment
—A work ethic one can only aspire to—
Bravely moving toward the other side,
Knowing not whether Spanish, English,
Or perhaps Polish is spoken there.

A body flattened and broken by love,
But unmarred by infection,
He will be missed internationally.

Al came in angrily waving the paper over his head the next morning.

"Where's *Whitman*?" he hollered, threatening to fire me. Herb, the obvious culprit, stifled a smirk.

As my obituaries got better, Al handed me occasional news items to cover as well. When I saw my first byline— "Peanut Butter Prices Not So Smooth" *by Steve Bardo*—I was ecstatic. It felt like I was starting to get somewhere, at least with writing. I was still perniciously isolated as far as romance went. After my initial conversation with Shirley, I had called almost daily, leaving many messages for her. Eventually, bowtie guy called back to say she was no longer employed at A.A. Raynor and had left no forwarding info. With Shirley beyond reach, I focused on writing and put her out of my mind best I could.

After the peanut butter article, Herb began inviting me to lunch at the Red Apple, a hearty Polish buffet just a block from work. One day, while wolfing down pierogi, kielbasa, and many cups of coffee, a well-put-together older woman named Sally joined us in the booth. I figured her for one of Herb's lady friends, but instead, she introduced herself as his literary agent. It turned out Herb, under the pseudonym "Earl Lockman," had published several hardboiled crime novels.

"Earl here named himself after a once-famous Chicago escape artist. I don't know what that says about him," Sally joked.

She went on to say that Herb had shared a few of my stories with her, and that she'd be willing to give me a little help if I was interested. I jumped at the chance.

Al let me take the typewriter home weekends until I could afford my own, which was going to be never, considering the Gazette's shitty pay. I followed Sally's editorial suggestions best I could and typed everything neatly as possible. Al wouldn't let me use the Gazette's Xerox, so I went to a twenty-four-hour print shop in the South Loop to make copies of my manuscripts.

I stuffed envelopes and licked stamps, sending the stories to literary journals on a list Sally had given me. She told me not to be discouraged if I got rejection letters. That sounded ridiculous to me. My stories were good. Sally and Herb had both said so. But several weeks after sending them around, rejections did start coming. They were all more or less the same.

Dear Mr. Bardo,
Blah blah… unfortunately… blah blah.
Sincerely,
Editor

It got so every time I saw, heard, or thought of the word *unfortunately*, I wanted to punch somebody in the nose. When I mentioned the problem to Herb, he told me to get over it or find something else to do with my life.

As winter set in, I began visiting the funerals of people I had obituarized. I'd been half-hoping to find Shirley working at one of the funeral parlors. But it was more than that, more than her. I was searching for a sense of purpose, too.

During that time, I also stopped writing short stories and sending them around. Instead, I put my efforts toward a new series of sideline obits that I called "Pre-obituaries of the Unfortunate." It all started with Herman Lutkus, a man with no known relatives or friends, whose employer—much as in the case with Diggy—had paid a funeral home to host a memorial that no one would attend. I know because I *did* attend.

> <u>For Herman Lutkus</u>
> He moved from one town to the next
> Haunted, lonely, sullen, vexed
> Determined not to stop for long
> Nor to look at what was wrong
> But he slowed a bit with age each year
> As did the demons that followed near
> They arrived together, broken down
> At an old folks' home, in an old folks' town
> Where aged demons' and mens' alike
> Minds again turn childlike
> And dissolve into demented goo
> Herman's did, ours will too.

After Herman, I dropped the corny couplet style and began writing my pre-obits as prose. Horror stories, really. Gathering info on the deceased each day, I extrapolated on the basic biographic details provided by local death venues to invent horrible, tragic lives that could only come to horrible, tragic ends. In the beginning, I focused on the protagonist's life alone, but later traced histories back two or three generations, showing how a given family's bad karma culminated in one descendant's particularly gruesome life, though only hinting at what their death might entail.

Writing the pre-obituaries may have deepened my depression, but at least I was writing.

One late January morning, as I was making my rounds, I dialed up a North Side funeral parlor and was surprised to hear a familiar female on the other end.

"White-boy old suit?" she asked, recognizing me as well.

In a moment of brazenness, or maybe desperation, I asked if we could meet in person to discuss "obituary information." An embarrassment-echo of my words caused me to move the mouthpiece while I cringed. But amazingly, after a moment of silence, Shirley asked where I lived. When I told her, she invited me to meet after work at The Artful Dodger, an arty dive right around the corner from my apartment. I wouldn't have expected her to know about a place like that, though I'm not sure what I expected from her. When I arrived, I found her chatting up the bartender. By her slurred speech, I assumed she'd been there awhile. I hadn't expected that either.

"Where's the old suit, white boy?" She asked.

Where's the kind lady I met at Diggy's memorial? I wondered.

Whatever I was hoping to get from Shirley that night, I didn't. Except the sex.

After that first encounter, we established a bi-weekly routine of getting hammered and going back to my place. All of our time together was either spent in bars or in my bed. In the mornings, when I awoke, she was always gone. *Incredible work ethic*, I thought in the beginning, but as she continued to avoid me during daylight hours, and never once invited me to her place, I became suspicious. Another troubling issue with Shirley was that she didn't allow our conversations to venture into personal matters. If I caught her in a near-sober moment and tried to discuss anything of importance, she would push me away. The only deep slice she shared that whole time was about being adopted by a white couple who ran a funeral parlor in St. Paul, Minnesota.

Carrie used to tell me I had abandonment issues. It was clear Shirley did too. I hoped it was something we could work through together.

One night, while Shirley was passed out in my bed, I opened her purse and found two pieces of ID that shared the same address: 2325 N. California Ave. Apt. One. It was just a mile and a half from my place. I copied it down.

When I woke up the next morning, Shirley was gone, per usual, but I felt sadder than usual about it. On my dresser, a dusty novel with the funeral sticker poking out from between pages reminded me I hadn't read or written a thing since I began seeing Shirley. Snatching the sticker from the book, I went to the kitchen to make coffee. The smell of the dark brew made me nauseous. I downed a beer in its place and headed for the door.

Walking toward Shirley's apartment, I held the orange sticker in front of me like a divining rod, waffling between Plan A: Bringing flowers, confessing my love, and asking her to move in with me. And Plan B: Giving an angry ultimatum to either work out her issues or find someone else to toy with.

I arrived, flowerless, half an hour later, and saw Shirley's car parked out front. A big white guy wearing a security guard getup happened to be entering the building just then. I snuck up behind and watched as he turned a key in the deadbolt of apartment one. Once he was inside, I entered the building and put my ear to the door he had just walked through. There was a lot of yelling. I didn't catch all of it, but I got the gist.

As I left, it seemed the sidewalks, more than my own feet, were carrying me home. But they weren't taking me south to my basement apartment in Bucktown, the home with the bed I'd been sharing with Shirley. Instead, they carried me north toward an earlier dwelling—a place I had hoped never to visit again. Block by block, as if traveling in both the wrong cardinal direction and the wrong direction of time, years of manufactured maturity and one-dimensional reinvention fell away until I was just a jittery, little kid wandering the streets, waiting for the next terrible thing to happen.

The window of our old apartment was open when I got there. I could almost hear Loraine hollering from the other side. The memory of her generated a rage in me that—probably for the first time in my life—was stronger than the fear she triggered. As I stood staring at the window, the words "Deuce Hood", followed by a sudden pain in my shoulder pulled me out of the flashback. I ducked as the next projectile came toward me. When the lone rock-chucker realized I wasn't such an easy target, his teenage voice went up an octave, his shouts suddenly aimed at his crew instead of me. I was faster than him and knew my way around those buildings better than anyone. By the time the others arrived, I had him on the ground, three face punches deep.

Running from the Lathrop Homes, I turned back again and again. Not for the gangbangers trailing me, but to see the bookmark I'd stuck on that old building fade into a little orange dot.

When I returned to the Gazette several days later, Herb didn't bother looking up. Dolores turned away from her work just long enough to point a bony finger at the supply closet where the typewriter had come from. Al came out of his office and looked at me a moment. In an eerily quiet voice, he said,

"Good luck, kid."

This whole story, the one I've been telling here, has been a sideline, an "unfortunate pre-obituary." Except in my case, it's all true. The signs of my fate were always there, poking and prodding, trying to get my attention. I don't know how or why I didn't see them. I suppose that's just how it is with people—staggering around blindly, grasping at any little flicker of light, hoping it will lead somewhere fantastic.

As far as the real obituary goes, I left it in the typewriter. Who knows, maybe that one will make it to print.

10.

The Little Library

Walking into a twenty-four-hour print shop, Young Man hears a door slam and lock behind him. A shadowy figure drags him toward a massive copy machine, opens the copier's coffin-shaped lid, and indicates for him to lie face down. Young Man glimpses his own reflection in the glass as he does so, but, horrifyingly, where his face should be, there are only words. Young Man twists and turns as the extreme pressure of the lid compacts him inside the machine. A whirring sound accompanied by blinding white light overcomes Young Man's senses as he's sucked into the copier and churned out—sentence by sentence, page by page—onto letter-sized paper. A human existence condensed into black and white.

His now flat, manuscript self, his pages, are snatched from the machine's tray and further formed, glued, bound, and covered. When the metamorphosis is complete, he's placed on a cart and wheeled down a long corridor.

"Home sweet home, New Title," the cart-pusher says, arriving at a glass-doored cement box.

Shoved onto a cramped shelf between other books, he tries shouting that he doesn't belong here, that he's a human being, not a book. But as the door to the little library closes, the speechless script previously known as Young Man, now referred to as New Title, begins to lose hope of returning to his former, corporeal self.

For a time, all is quiet in the little library. The glaring hall light and the immovability of New Title and his neighbors are all there is. As time passes, though, New Title notices words and sentences coming toward him like a distress signal.

"Don't you hear them? Can't *anyone* hear them? You have to let them in!" it says.

New Title can't reply, but the voice, which seems to be coming from a book behind him, is discernibly feminine. And now that she mentions it, he can hear it too.

Snakes, he thinks. *Venomous snakes that have nothing to bite.*

New Title recalls the snake house at the Lincoln Park Zoo. How children taunted the creatures, trying to make them show their fangs. How the exotic reptiles writhed irritably around each other in little cement boxes.

"Not snakes. It's my parents. They're calling through the radiator!" the voice cries.

Can she read my thoughts? New Title wonders.

"It's not your fault," she says. "Not everyone has as many ears as I do."

As her crying slows, she whispers confidentially, "I've got ears that hear the words, ears that hear between the words, and ears that hear the bottomless pit. That's why I'm here. It's just an ear infection."

New Title wishes he could see all her ears.

Another book, immediately to New Title's left, begins chatting him up as well. This time with a man's voice.

"When I fell off the roof, my head bounced on the cement. Just like a basketball. Bom bom bom. I wouldn't sue the boss. Everyone said I should sue, but I'm not like that. Then, right outta the sky, my hammer came down. Hit me in the solar plexus. That's below the heart. Solar means sun. When it shines, you get heartburn. I get heartburn a lot. It's these shiny pills. My head feels like a basketball. Do you watch sports? I used to watch sports after work. But then I fell off the sun. Don'tcha worry 'bout me, though. No, sir. I'll get up again. Hehe. Can't keep me on the bench for long. I used to play for the Phoenix Suns…"

Then, to his right, New Title hears a book talking in images alone. *Must be a picture book*, he thinks.

Suddenly, the sounds and wails of other library inhabitants fill the air: self-important autobiographies, rhyming children's books, hard-boiled crime stories, wordy academic tomes, laughing joke books, explicit romance novels, solemn manifestos, tear-jerking family dramas, and many, many mysteries—all the types of books one would expect at a regular lending library. But this place, New Title begins to realize, is for titles that have been taken out of circulation—a little library for books that no one cares to read.

Occasionally, a terrifying creature—a massive head with hands but no body—peers through the glass door looking for a particular volume. When the heads pop up, fear and anxiety, like bookworms, spread from title to title. No one wants to be rummaged through by the bodiless monsters, but there's nowhere to hide from their horrible hands. One by one, day by day, New Title's neighbors are yanked from the concrete container and whisked to an unknown place. The books that return, if they're able to communicate, tell terrible tales of "the editing room." New Title's pages tremble at the thought of it.

Soon, the big heads come for New Title too. The first time they take him, he's placed on a cart and wheeled to a brightly lit room where several frowning heads with small rubber hands are waiting hungrily. They turn him this way and that, jotting down notes about when and where he was printed as well as the condition of his cover, binding, and pages. The largest head in the room thumbs momentarily through New Titles chapters and then sticks something sharp inside him.

A bookmark, New Title thinks as he drifts off to sleep.

When he regains consciousness, New Title, realizing he's been reshelved in the little library, hears other books gossiping all around him. One of his neighbors finally asks,

"How was the assessment? Did you get a price tag?"

When New Title doesn't respond, the books discuss among themselves what value, if any, the appraisers might have placed upon him. An old woman's voice chimes in cheerily,

"If you're given a high value, they'll send you to the *bookstore.*"

As time passes, New Title is brought out for evaluation by other giant heads. Book critics comment on problems with his plot structure and character development. They shake their big, horrid heads in complaint, as if New Title weren't even there, comparing him to other poorly written works they'd read recently—ones, like him, not meant for public consumption. The only benign remark New Title hears during the entire story inspection is that his symbolism is "somewhat interesting."

The distress of being removed and reviewed, scrutinized, and scribbled on becomes the main topic of New Title's inner narration. He considers how the oversized heads focus only on the books' problems, never appreciating or enjoying their pages just as they are.

But maybe that's just how it is with literature experts, he thinks.

One day, New Title hears two heads pushing carts in opposite directions stop to talk in front of the little library. One, an appraiser, comments that he can't shelve a particular book because it has no binding at all.

"It's just a bunch of loose pages," it says.

The other, a critic, complains that he just read a book with "too many characters."

Those titles, they agree, will have to be sent to another place—a bin out back for books beyond mending or editing.

Are they talking about me? New Title frets.

As he contemplates his fate, a hand reaches inside the box and drops off a book no one had heard from in a while. Its cover is badly torn, and it appears much slimmer than before.

"My god, they've removed entire chapters from the wretch," someone says.

New Title wonders if the heads have noticed, as his neighbors have, how voluminous his own manuscript has become lately, taking up more shelf space than the others. It's burdensome having stories repopulate his pages—as if returning him to an earlier, unabridged edition of himself—while other books are reworked and emptied of their original meaning. The chapters, now filling him from cover to cover, are about people. Real people that New Title assumes he once knew. It's almost as if they're inside him, writing the words themselves, filling in his lost pieces.

The haunting harmony that moaned alongside Diggy bounced hard off the tenement bricks, ricocheting and reverberating toward him.

Whistlin' shotgun. Stairs don't end
Whistlin' shotgun. Stairs go down
Whistlin' whistlin'. Too many peoples
Whistlin' shotgun. Babies in the ground

How could this girl, this guitar goddess, follow the bluesman—who never played the same note twice—through every riff, run, and note bend?

Two giant heads appear in the window, stopping New Title mid-paragraph. They pluck him off the shelf, place him on a cart, and roll him down an incredibly long corridor. Eventually, they arrive in a large, colorful room full of shiny plants and soft furniture. A head with a kind, smiling face—one he's never seen—speaks directly to him.

"Hi Steve, it's Sally. Your agent... can he *hear* me?"

One of the cart-pushers nods.

"I came to tell you that 'Diggy' was optioned. Your story will be a movie, Steve!"

New Title narrates in the smiling head's direction, but she doesn't seem able to read his thoughts like the books do.

"It's been fast-tracked into production. This is great news for you...."

He tries harder, but it's no use.

"Christ, what have you got him goofed on?"

As a frowning, floating head signifies it's time to go, New Title feels dampness dripping down his cover, pooling on the cart.

"He's not crazy!" Sally yells, as the door buzzer sounds and they begin wheeling him back down the long corridor.

11.

Diggy

"Lonzo, I done tol' ya' 'bout hollin' in them fields. Time to pack yo' thangs and git, bwah," the straw boss said.

By 1934, at nineteen years old, Alonzo had been fired from every cotton farm between Vicksburg and Greenville. And every time he was let go, it was for the same reason: his singing. It wasn't that he was a bad singer, particularly. In fact, it could be said Alonzo carried a tune better than most. And it wasn't that he couldn't follow the songs the other workers sang. Alonzo knew every field holler that'd ever been moaned, groaned, hummed, or strummed. And it wasn't that he sang too warbly, or out of time, or couldn't harmonize, or stole the lead part. Nonetheless, there was something about Alonzo's vocalizations—and most everyone who heard him agreed—that was just plain off-putting.

Because it was hard to put an exact finger on the problem, the other field hands looked to supernatural explanations for the unsettling singing. Some said the young man was hexed. Others said he had a bad spirit following him. A few went so far as to suggest that Alonzo himself was a phantasm of some sort or another. Whatever the case, when Alonzo joined in on group hollers, the other workers became so ill-at-ease that they walked off the job, leaving behind hoes, plows, and mules, or cotton sacks and baskets, depending on the season. Of course, Alonzo knew better than to share in the songs, but sooner or later, he just couldn't keep from belting them out.

"It feel like sumpin' cookin' way down in the groun'. Bubblin' like burlin' water. I feels it comin' and comin'. Into my feets and laigs and all the way up til it rise in my throat and come out my mouth," he explained to Henrietta, the only person he'd ever met who appreciated his singing.

"God done gifted you with sumpin' this worl' ain't never seen befo', 'Lonzo," she often told him.

While the couple packed their few possessions into cardboard suitcases, Henrietta's older brother Thomas, who'd gotten Alonzo the job, came to the door of their tenant shack.

"Look-a-here, 'Lonzo. Heard tell they needs a gravedigger at Nitta Yuma Cemetery. That 'bout the onliest place you ain't gwine botha' no bodies which yo' sangin'."

Henrietta and Alonzo ambled off solemnly in the late September sun. When they finally reached 61 Highway, they thumbed a ride south to Panther Burn, walking the last few miles to Nitta Yuma. At the general store, Alonzo told an old white lady at the counter he was interested in the gravedigger job. After squinting and tsking at the Black couple for a full minute, the old lady hollered for her husband. The man, known to everyone as Mister Charlie, came in from the backroom and walked around Alonzo as if inspecting a side of beef.

"Where yo' last place of employment was?" Mister Charlie asked, skeptically.

"Simmons Farm."

"Uh *huh*. And if I call Bubba Simmons on the telephone, what he's gwine tell me 'boutcha, bwah?"

"Sposin' he say other folk don't likes the way I holla."

"Bad sanger, huh? Prolly ain't the foist one 'ol Bubba let go fo' that. I reckon you ain't gwine botha nobody hollin' out in the sem-a-tree," Mister Charlie chuckled.

Due to rumors of hauntings, Mister Charlie had been having a hard time keeping a cemetery groundskeeper. As such, he looked the young man dead in the eye and asked, "Ain't 'fraid a no ghosts, *is ya*?"

Alonzo shook his head no and followed Mister Charlie to an outbuilding on the cemetery grounds where the old man pulled out a rickety shovel.

"Six down, eight-by-three across," Mister Charlie said, pointing to a plot under a tree.

Without negotiating wage, hours, or other details, Alonzo accepted the shovel and watched Mister Charlie shuffle back toward the general store.

Nightfall had come by the time Alonzo finished the digging. Henrietta brought sandwiches made by Mister Charlie's wife, Miss Dora.

"They say you gots the job 'Lonzo," she said cheerily.

The couple was too tired to go in search of lodging, instead opting to sleep in the cemetery that night. Alonzo sang her a song that had come to him while digging that day. He called it "Deepen Your Grave."

Wide and deep. Awake too long.
Deepen your grave. Time to sleep.
Down and dirty. Played yo' cards.
Six feet down a righteous home.
Deepen your grave. Wide and deep.

Henrietta clapped when he finished.

"Oh, 'Lonzo, they need to make records on yo' sangin'… like Charlie Patton. The world need to *hear* you," she said.

If it wasn't for Henrietta, Alonzo thought, *I wouldn't make it in this world a-tall."*

The couple settled into a small, dilapidated shack on the outskirts of town—one of many owned by Mister Charlie. Henrietta took work in the main house helping the chief caretaker, Miss Pearlean, with the grandchildren and the cleaning, though not the cooking—the kitchen was Pearlean's purview alone. Unable to become pregnant herself, Henrietta gave her motherlove to Mister Charlie and Miss Dora's grandbabies, doting on them as if they were her own.

When Alonzo and Henrietta needed supplies, they were purchased directly from Mister Charlie, who added the cost of groceries, clothes, and sundry items to his "tally"—a powerful sheaf of papers he wagged at them whenever the couple asked for wages.

A few weeks into the job, Alonzo got himself a second-hand Sears Roebuck guitar. The "Stella", purchased a year prior as a Christmas gift for Mister Charlie's eldest grandson, Jo-Jo—only to find out the boy was more interested in piano—had only five strings on it when it came into Alonzo's possession. Mister Charlie scribbled a number and the word "guitar" into the tally—another debt for his gravedigger to work off.

Working in the cemetery, Alonzo was able to sing freely without objection from any person, living or dead. Not only did he get no complaints about his singing, it felt to him like the people six feet down eight-by-three across were encouraging, joining, and, at times, even singing through him. As such, he began to suspect that the music percolating through him each day was in no part his own creation. The rumblings that became bubbles that became feelings that became songs, he reckoned, were none other than the moans of buried people, beckoning him to sing out to the living world on their behalves. The musical kinship Alonzo found with Nitta Yuma's dead brought a sense of well-being previously experienced only through his relationship with Henrietta. But more than that, Henrietta was no longer the only one who needed him.

At night, when he came home, Alonzo transposed the graveyard tunes as best he could onto his five-stringed Stella. Henrietta danced and clapped along to the guitar music, sometimes finding a harmony part to warble atop Alonzo's moans. Though it was all good fun, the song-filled evenings weren't nearly enough entertainment for Henrietta. As such, whenever they had a little spending money, she cajoled Alonzo into taking her out juking.

While Henrietta cut loose drinking and dancing at local juke joints, fish frys, and Saturday night suppers, Alonzo kept a close eye on the fancy fingerwork of the leading blues guitarists who entertained them. Though many were skilled, the most gifted pickers in the area—to Alonzo's sensibilities—were Bo Carter and Skip James. The two elder bluesmen got used to the younger man hanging around with his cheap guitar and pretty girlfriend, offering him pointers on how to play when they weren't flirting with Henrietta. Though both Bo and Skippy told Alonzo he needed to put a sixth string on his Stella, he never did add the high E.

Alonzo practiced daily over the next two years, becoming proficient enough at plucking his five-string to attract followers of his own. Two local teenagers in particular—Hezekiah Bolden, known to everyone as "Slow Drag," and another named Noobie Youngblood—came around regularly to find Alonzo picking and singing on his day off in a remote section of the Nitta Yuma Cemetery.

Noobie and Slow Drag, being more ambitious than Alonzo, not only copied the gravedigger's odd tunings and guitar licks, they also took his strange songs and rearranged them, making them more palatable for a listening audience.

In time, Slow Drag Bolden became a sought-after musician in his own right, recording versions of Alonzo's "Whistlin' Shotgun" and "Deepen Your Grave" for the Okeh Records label.

Several months after Slow Drag Bolden's recording session, Henrietta and Alonzo were sipping spo-dee-odee in a roadhouse outside of Rolling Fork when the jukebox needle dropped on Slow Drag's single.

"That was *yo'* song, 'Lonzo!" She repeated several times, as they drove home in a beat-up T Model pickup that Alonzo was paying off slowly—like everything else he "owned"—by working for Mister Charlie.

"That boy just doin' his own thang," Alonzo said of his imitator.

"It's time to make yo' *own* records. You gots to see Mr. H.C. Speirs in Jackson. Thas what Bo 'n them say."

Not wanting to displease Henrietta, Alonzo made the trip to town the following weekend.

H.C. happened to be standing out front of his phonograph store on Farish Street as the two pulled up. When he saw the guitar come out of the T Model, H.C. offered Alonzo the opportunity to do an impromptu audition right there on the sidewalk. The unusual sounds emitting from the young man and his cheap guitar were so confusing to H.C., he was certain it was either a new fad in race music or else he was standing before a one-of-a-kind musical prodigy. Not wanting to miss a great opportunity, H.C. set up a demo session immediately, offering Alonzo a bottle of store-bought whiskey and ten dollars in exchange for his signature on a contract. Henrietta took the bottle from Alonzo—who didn't drink much anyway—and had a few nips, proudly watching while her man sang into the white man's machine.

After recording a few of Alonzo's graveyard-inspired songs and finding out the young man was, in fact, a gravedigger by trade, H.C. marked down the artist's name as "Diggy" Nubbit before placing the acetates into shipping boxes marked for his contacts at Victor, Paramount, and Brunswick.

When the couple left the backroom of the phonograph shop, Henrietta, who had by then finished half the bottle of booze, whisked Alonzo into the T Model truck and proceeded to kiss him until there was no place left on him to kiss. Alonzo was more than ready to drive home after the day's excitements, but Henrietta wanted to get a gander at Farish Street's people and shops. By the time the stores closed, Alonzo was toting a hat in a hatbox, a pair of shoes, and a few smaller purchases he'd made for Henrietta with H.C.'s money. The couple shared tamales and pig ear sandwiches at the end of the day while listening to a blind blues singer busk nearby. Alonzo tossed his last dime to the blind performer as they walked off.

Every weekend that followed, Henrietta asked Alonzo to drive back and see if H.C. had news about his recording career.

"He know where to find me, Sugar," Alonzo said, reassuringly.

A month later, when Henrietta finally convinced him to return to Jackson, they found the phonograph shop closed and shuttered. A man cleaning the sidewalk in front of Speir's store said H.C. had retired from recording and was no longer actively pursuing musical talent.

"The last man come through here done broke Mister H.C. machine," the cleanup man said.

"Who that *was*?" Henrietta asked, nervously.

"Them *big* rekkid comp'nies? Every sint Mister H.C. sent that crazy song 'round. Uh-*uh*. They ain't want nuttin' do wit' him. Onliest thang he talk about for weeks. Some country fool name-a *Diggy Nubbit*."

On the way home, Henrietta told herself it must be some other country fool with the same last name. But, no matter the case, she knew they'd never return to H.C.'s store.

When the pain of the Jackson trip eventually wore off, Henrietta, thinking it was a cute name, took to calling Alonzo "Diggy." The moniker caught on so quickly, it was as if Nitta Yuma's residents had never known the gravedigger by any other name. Alonzo embraced the title wholeheartedly, for not only was his vocation carried in it, so was his true calling in life—digging up and voicing the memories of the dead. Along with the new name came a new confidence.

Over the next few years, Diggy continued digging graves and doing other odd jobs for Mister Charlie. The work was stable, if not well-paying. Henrietta became Mister Charlie and Miss Dora's chief housekeeper when Miss Pearlean grew too old to keep house. The slight raise in salary afforded Henrietta the purchase of an occasional blues record to play on her very own wind-up gramophone—another hand-me-down from the main house scribbled in the boss's book.

When the big war came, Mister Charlie spoke to his friends at the local draft board on Diggy's behalf. The young man was too much needed by him to go off and battle "the Nazzys and Japs."

"Y'all take a look an' see. My Diggy ain't no fighter," he proclaimed, passing around bottles of locally made hooch while parading his gravedigger around the Elks Lodge.

Diggy wasn't drafted.

Just after the war, in early 1946, Mister Charlie died suddenly of a heart attack. It was Diggy who dug the hole in Nitta Yuma cemetery, lowered him down, and poured every last shovel of thick delta dirt over the ornate box that would be Mr. Charlie's final abode.

For days after the funeral, Diggy sat alone near Mister Charlie's plot, weeping his way through the many songs that bubbled through him. He wasn't particularly distraught over his boss's passing, but dead-Mister-Charlie felt so much regret for how he'd spent his time above the earth, he wouldn't let Diggy rest either—a tiring taskmaster, even in the afterlife.

Within a month of the burial, the old man's eldest, Charles Jr., moved his mama into a newly built house up in Memphis near his own, selling off much of his daddy's landholdings, including the general store, the family home, and the cemetery. Diggy and Henrietta received no severance when they were let go, but on the other hand, no one made them pay off Mister Charlie's interminable tally, which, for the boss's children, was just another illegible ledger lying about the old man's office.

With nothing left for them in Nitta Yuma, Henrietta insisted they move to Jackson. She was certain that with the many barrelhouses, jukes, and theaters the metropolitan area had to offer, Diggy could secure employment as a professional musician if he would only put his mind to it.

After finding temporary accommodations for himself and Henrietta in a rooming house off Farish Street, Diggy landed a job in the city's historic Greenwood Cemetery. Though the expectations for groundskeeping were more challenging than at Nitta Yuma—which left Diggy less time for music—the pay was quite a bit better. With Diggy's increase in wages, Henrietta was afforded a break from work. She made fast friends in the neighborhood among people, like herself, who enjoyed drinking and dancing. There, too, were more men around Jackson since the war ended, including more bluesmen to play the local barrelhouses, jukes, and theaters. Ever fond of music-making men, Henrietta found herself in their company on weekends and even weekdays while Diggy was busy digging.

"Elmo' and Sonny Boy tol' me they's a new music comp'ny right here in Jackson called Sho' Fire Records. You *best* do them a tryout, Diggy," Henrietta insisted.

Not wanting to displease Henrietta, Diggy took his five-string to the address she'd given him for Surefire Records, which turned out to be a furniture store just a stone's throw from H.C. Spier's old place. The shop's owners, Alvin and Roberta Bascom, sat at a cheap-looking dinette set in the storefront window while they listened to the young man play a few licks.

"Can't imagine anyone dancing to *that*," Mrs. Bascom opined.

"Play a lil' more, son. Put some *feelin'* into it," Mr. Bascom encouraged.

Diggy smiled in acceptance of the white folk's remarks, but his feeling was already fully in the music, same as ever.

Mr. Bascom stood and walked around the unusual guitar man, nodding his head and scratching his chin.

"Berta, call them rhythm boys. Let's try it out."

Mrs. Bascom humphed and stormed off to make the call.

That afternoon, in a warehouse next to the furniture store, Diggy set up to record with a drummer and bass player. Hoping for a more modern sound than what he'd heard that morning, Mr. Bascom replaced Diggy's acoustic with a brand new National Aristocrat electric guitar.

"This gi'tah have 'lectricity *in it*?" Diggy asked.

"Don't fret none. You isn't gonna git zapped," Mr. Bascom assured, as he watched the young picker remove a string and detune the instrument.

The bass player adjusted his own strings to meet Diggy's while sharing looks with the drummer. It was hard for either of them to find a groove behind the strange country boy, but somehow, they managed to track four songs. At the end of the session, Mr. Bascom paid the rhythm section while telling Diggy he would "receive compensation if-and-when albums are sold."

A few months later, Surefire printed copies of what Mr. Bascom deemed to be Diggy's two best tracks: "Sweet Red Dirt" and "Deepen Your Grave." The rhythmically disjointed songs were, to say the least, unsettling to Mrs. Bascom.

"Sugar plum, you never know what these coloreds gonna like," Mr. Bascom said.

Berta was certain no one would dance to it.

On the day Diggy's singles were set out for display in the record department—a small area between the cash register and vanities—Henrietta visited Bascom Furniture, same as she'd done every Friday since the recording session. But this time, walking in and finding a record with Diggy's name on it, she nearly fainted. Mrs. Bascom ushered Henrietta out of the store with a free copy of the disc, saying,

"No cash changes hands 'til we sell at least fifty copies. *Fifty*. Hear?"

Henrietta ran straight right home and dropped the 78RPM single onto her out-of-date wind-up gramophone. Proud of her man and his accomplishment, Henrietta spent the rest of the afternoon buzzard loping, snake hipping, and shimmying to his otherworldly music.

The next day, Mr. Bascom drove Diggy's record around to the few radio stations within a hundred-mile radius that played Black music. With a smile and a pint of whisky, he handed off Diggy's single to any disc jockey he thought might give it a spin.

On the way home, Mr. Bascom switched on the radio in his Desoto sedan. Flipping the dial, he landed on Vicksburg's WQBC just as the new blues DJ, Jerome Stampley, was announcing the next song.

"…and that was Robert Pet-a-way sanging 'bout them "Catfish Blues." Right now, we got us a new blues cat name-a Diggy Nubbit makin' his debut on Sho' Fire Records. Give a listen to *Sweet Red Dirt*."

Mr. Bascom, congratulating himself on his business acumen, cranked up the volume as his latest recording came crackling across the airwaves. But as Diggy's opening licks wafted through the Desoto's speakers, something curious happened. A loud pop followed by a spark emitting from the dashboard nearly made Bascom turn into a ditch. Then, with a fizzle, the radio went off.

"Jesus H…damn car's only a *year* old!" Mr. Bascom hollered, flipping knobs and banging on the apparatus.

While considering the exact words he'd let loose on Hollis "Mister Deals" Moore when he arrived at the Desoto dealership, Mr. Bascom became aware of large plumes of smoke in the near distance. He squinted at the sky and then at his radio. Somehow, the two problems seemed interconnected. When he brought his attention back to the thick brown billows darkening the air in front of him, it became clear they were emanating from the direction of Farish Street. Though he repeated to himself, *couldn't possibly be, couldn't possibly, couldn't…* he raced toward the store anyway.

Turning onto his block, Mr. Bascom saw flames jumping behind a large crowd of gawkers. Jumping out of the Desoto and pushing his way through the people, he found Berta crying on the shoulder of a policeman. The fire brigade managed to keep the blaze from spreading to the rest of Farish Street.

By 1951, Henrietta was no longer content living in Jackson. Her brother, Thomas, had moved North to Memphis and had written her of the better pay, better entertainment, and overall better life up in the big city. Henrietta, desperate to make the move, persuaded Diggy to quit his job and pack up the T-Model. The notion that he could carve out a place for himself in the blues world still hadn't left her, and, as she'd told him many times, there was no better place than Memphis to do just that.

Settling in with Thomas and his family, Diggy hunted for work at Memphis cemeteries while Henrietta got busy making new friends. After a particularly long night of revelry on Beale Street, Henrietta stumbled into her brother's living room and woke Diggy, who was snoring softly on the couch.

"Hollin' Wolf and them say you needs to go to *Ron-Jon Records!*"

With Henrietta as his only anchor in the world of the living, Diggy agreed to most every request she made. They both knew that without her, he was liable to forget ordinary tasks like bathing, eating properly, and cashing work checks. And so it was that on his first day off after starting at Memphis's Elmwood Cemetery, Diggy drove his guitar downtown and took his place at the end of a long line of musicians passing bottles and practicing songs in preparation for their Ron Jon Records tryouts.

After three hours of inching slowly through the old-theater-repurposed-as-recording-studio, Diggy was asked to enter an office and perform for two well-dressed, middle-aged white men. He closed his eyes and breathed into the earth below him, letting his fingers and voice find their way into the music. When he finished singing and opened his eyes, Diggy watched as the two men scratched their heads and chins, repeating the phrases,

"Wasn't that something." and "That was something, alright."

After a few minutes whispering closely about the "highly unique performer," one of the men smiled and offered Diggy a contract along with the promise of a twenty-dollar cash payment upon completion of his first recording. Diggy hoped it would make Henrietta happy.

A week later, at the scheduled recording time, Diggy arrived at the theater to find the men he had met previously arranging microphones while a few bleary-eyed musicians smoked in a corner.

"Baris, get a saxophone on this one. It's got a be-bop to it," Ronald Jonson, the label owner, said as Diggy began picking his first number.

Baris assembled Ron-Jon's usual rhythm section, plus a piano and saxophone. The band warmed up with a few snappy numbers, sounding tight and soulful. When everything else was set, Baris cued Diggy to start playing. Some of the musicians looked upon the presentation curiously, others perplexedly. The drummer let out a laugh. Though all the studio musicians were top-notch, nothing they did aligned with Diggy's sound and no suggestions they offered helped to straighten him out. The off-kilter rhythms they recorded that day weren't exactly blues or jazz, nor were they the new rhythm and blues music that was becoming so popular. Baris, not knowing what to call it, agreed it had "a be-bop to it," but no one knew what to do with the recordings when the session was over.

Because the lyrics and music were so unusual, Ronald thought one of the singles might earn money as a novelty song. He printed a hundred copies of the single—Side-A: "Whistlin' Shotgun" Side-B: "Wide and Deep"—and spread them around Black record stores and radio stations in the greater Memphis area.

Finding a copy of the newly pressed record set out on her dining room table one evening, Ronald's wife, Betty, gave it a spin on their home hi-fi set. While the strange song plunked, and shambled, and tramped along, Betty found herself shifting positions—from standing, to sitting, to slumping, to crawling on all fours—as she became burdened by a lead-like weight in her head and chest—a heaviness unlike anything she'd previously experienced. At the conclusion of "Whistlin' Shotgun," as the hi-fi needle skipped in the runout groove, Betty collapsed into her bed. And there she remained there for the next ten days without uttering a word.

The family physician, Dr. Morris, diagnosed Betty with severe melancholia and recommended she be moved posthaste to Gailor Memorial, a residential psychiatric facility where he held a part-time position. Ronald, distressed about his wife's condition, drank to excess while taking sedatives prescribed by Dr. Morris. Another Ron-Jon record was never to be made.

Diggy and Henrietta, along with Thomas, followed the Black migration north as the 1950s progressed. From Memphis, they moved briefly to St. Louis and a little later, settled in Bronzeville on Chicago's Southside. Diggy found work at nearby Oak Woods Cemetery where, as always, he made himself familiar with the names and stories of the dead—not by reading books or obituaries, but by feeling and listening to the sounds arising inside himself as he heaved shovel after shovel of hard Chicago dirt over his shoulder. Each day, the desperate souls six down, eight-by-three across called up to him. Poets and politicians, mothers and children, workers and bosses, Soldiers of the Union and Confederacy—and even a few mob bosses—shouting each one louder than the other about the pain they'd experienced in life, and the even more painful state of being trapped in a dark, cold, semi-existence without a body or a loved one to comfort them. As he toiled tirelessly through the days, Diggy sang out the truths revealed to him by Oak Woods' dead, causing his co-workers to avoid him for the sake of their own well-being.

For her part, Henrietta was delighted with big city life. She made new acquaintances quickly and discovered that many old friends from down south were living in Bronzeville too. Though she still looked after Diggy—and continued to believe in his talents—Henrietta gave her "good loving" to the professional musicians who performed in Chicago's Southside bars and nightclubs. Diggy knew about the infidelities but never mentioned them, understanding that a big-hearted woman like Henrietta had too much love for just one man.

Though the couple had grown apart since arriving in Chicago, they still managed to spend every Sunday together. Most often, they went to "Jewtown," as the Maxwell Street

Market was known, to eat pork chop sandwiches, shop for sundry items, and most of all, to hear blues performed by the best down-home and big city artists of the genre.

On one such Sunday, while wading through street peddlers, bible preachers, buskers, and shoppers, the couple happened past an unusually quiet dirt lot. It was the only nook in the entire market where no item, ideology, or song was being peddled, preached or performed. There wasn't so much as a pair of dice being tossed in the garbage-cluttered dirt patch that sat between two vacant, crumbling tenements. As they got closer, Diggy noticed the area was not only devoid of activity; it was incredibly quiet, almost painfully so.

Struck with a sudden foreboding, Henrietta attempted to steer Diggy back toward the singers and hawkers behind them. But Diggy wouldn't budge. His breathing grew rapid, audible, as he released Henrietta's hand and lurched herky-jerkily toward the lot as if pulled by a magnet. When he reached the epicenter of the noiseless space, Diggy fell to his knees and put his ear to the ground.

"Diggy, this place ain't right. Stop foolin'. Come on, now!" Henrietta called, but Diggy didn't hear.

As she braced herself and took a step into the lot, a step toward her man, he suddenly sprang erect and reached his arms to the sky. The noises that issued from Diggy just then—without a single word of English in them—were so unfamiliar, they set Henrietta back on her heels. *Some kind of tongue-talking*, she thought. But the noises were more desperate, more agonized than anything she'd ever heard come out of church folk. A few passersby peeked at the curious display, though only peripherally. No one wanted to get close with eye, ear, or limb to the babbling "crazy man." No one, including Henrietta.

When the next Sunday came around, Diggy visited Maxwell Street alone. The following Sunday he did the same. It was unusual for anyone to come near him, but on the rare occasion someone did stumble into that strange space at the outer edge of the market, they had no clue what was happening, and Diggy—in part because he himself wasn't sure what was happening—had more sense than to try and explain. What he did know was that the "deep fire", as he called the spring of energy flowing up and into the backlot, came from much further below the earth's crust than six down, eight-by-three across. And the souls dwelling down there, "the fire folks," needed him, demanded more from him than anyone dead or alive ever had. Where the shallow-buried cemetery dead merely required Diggy's voice to sing out their stories, the fire folks took over his entire body to communicate information about Reality itself. The day Diggy first stepped into that little Maxwell Street lot, he became a living bridge between this world and another, sharing not only the fire folks' songs, but their way of being with the people above.

Week after week, taking his place above the deep fire, a dark light flowed through Diggy's throat, fingers, and feet, troubling its way into the souls of anyone who came near, showing them things about who and what they are, what this world actually is, that few could bear to see.

There were times even Diggy resisted the reflective force. On those rare occasions, when he turned away from the dark light, Diggy left the lot feeling lost, with senses dimmed and mind muddled. By contrast, when he stayed open to the deep fire and what it had to show, Diggy departed Maxwell Street Sunday evenings with heightened intuitions about the people, situations, living things, and even non-living things that presented themselves to him. It was as if the fire folks stayed with Diggy, guiding him moment by moment, step by step, bringing him to a greater understanding of the world and his place in it. There was no way he could give that up to be like other men, like other musicians. There was no way he could do that, not even for Henrietta.

When she finally left him to move in with Slow Drag Bolden—who had by then progressed from song-stealing to wife-stealing—Diggy was brokenhearted, but not broken of spirit. In his grief-stricken state, Diggy discovered a liberating truth about his life: the loneliness he had carried with him all his years wasn't his alone. It was, and always had been, shared by the fire folks. Somehow, just as he did for them, they sang out to their world on his behalf, too.

12.

Triple Feature

The Oriental was amazing back then. Always a triple feature. Three movies for a dollar—one kung fu, one horror, one softcore drama. It was the poor folks' theatre. The street drunks' theater. The prostitutes' and pimps' theater. The abandoned, runaway, and truant kids' theater.

There was a seating system at the Oriental everyone figured out pretty quick. Kids running wild up front. Make-out sessions and movie watchers in the middle. Drunks, homeless, and sex workers in the back. Steve always sat middle-front. Far enough from the souses, sleepers, and sexers, but not too close to the rowdy kids. Urine occasionally streamed down the slanted concrete floor from the back rows. He kept his feet propped on the chair in front to avoid the mess, wondering if the back-row pissers didn't want to miss the movie or were just too wasted to get up and use the toilet.

At intermission, Steve liked to wander up and down corridors, touching the sculpted walls, pillars, and railings. The heavy red curtain pulled back at each side of the screen smelled like cigars and looked to be a hundred years old.

Even the men's room seemed marvelous with its massive ornate urinals—almost too beautiful to piss in. Maybe the real reason so many people pissed on the floors, he figured. Sometimes Steve went treasure hunting, finding things people had dropped or left behind before the ushers got to them. Coins. Articles of clothing. Bottles of alcohol. Once he even found a wallet with a two-dollar bill and a driver's license. And if he was hungry, there were plenty of half-full buckets of popcorn lying around.

Though his father promised to pick him up later, Steve kept enough change on hand to catch the subway home when Ernie inevitably didn't show. On the twenty-five-minute rides from State and Randolph to Diversey and Sheffield, Steve imagined other passengers to be actors in a movie of his own creation:

She's following the killer off the train. When she finds out where he lives, she'll come back with her friends and burn his house down.

He belongs to a secret martial arts society and has vowed never to cause harm unless someone litters on the train.

The lovers are riding to the end of the line where no one can ever bother them again.

"Diversey," the conductor announces, interrupting Steve's reminiscing.

He tucks away the eulogy he's been preparing for Ernie's funeral and moves toward the door. Steve looks back at the other passengers as the train slows and runs the game one more time:

Eight-year-old boy shakes sleeping father, worrying he may have overdosed again.

Teenager acts tough, psyching himself up for first prison visit.

Hollywood screenwriter finds childhood memories waiting for him inside Chicago train car twenty years later.

Too bad they don't show movies at the Oriental anymore, he thinks.

Stories

March 15th

"We got him," the cop said proudly, stuffing me in the back of a brand new '81 Crown Vic. It had that nauseating new car smell mixed with sweat, stale coffee, and Italian beef. They must've just had lunch.

As we started driving, the pudgy plainclothesman in the passenger seat turned to face me, shooting a look I had come to call the "glare of the conqueror." I stared back. When he saw I wasn't so easily shaken, he let out a dismissive snort, faced forward, and radioed it in:

"Suspect matches description. White male. Thirties. Medium build. Facial scar..."

Apparently, I resembled a burglar known for stealing high-end tchotchkes from old folks' homes in the area. It was the third time I'd been picked up that month. I knew the process well:

1. Cops spot me, excited to be the ones to nab the "bric-a-brac bandit."

2. They run my ID and find out I'm not their guy.

3. They get mad at me for being the wrong guy and try to find something else to hold me on.

4. I walk a mile and a half home from the precinct, hoping not to get picked up by some other jag-off cop.

But this time was different. For one thing, they didn't run my ID. I had mistakenly left my wallet in another pair of pants when I went to work that morning and—though I told them where it was—those gung-ho cops weren't about to turn around and take me home. Another difference was where they took me. Downtown, 11th and State, not the local cop shop. I figured these clowns were planning to march me into the chief's office looking for a promotion.

When we got there, they yanked me out of the car so hard I almost fell on my face. Definitely harsher treatment than usual. Inside, I was printed and then tossed in a holding cell.

The idea of going to prison for a crime I didn't commit had been a fear of mine as a youngster. A common fear, I had assumed, for guys like me who grew up poor in Chicago—we'd all known people put away for doing little to nothing wrong. By 1981, at thirty years old, the Chicago P.D. had just about ground the fear of mistaken identity out of me with their unintentional "exposure therapy." But as I sat in the basement of police headquarters that morning, the old anxiety crept back in. It didn't help that a guy two cells over kept yelling, "I ain't *did* nuttin'," every ten minutes or so.

After what seemed like hours, I was led to a room with loud lights, a table, a few chairs, and a long two-way mirror—an interrogation room, just like in the movies.

"I'm not the bandit and you know it," I said.

"Alright, Jerry," a tall, chiseled-faced cop said, pointing for me to sit down.

It was odd to be called by my childhood nickname. I'd been known as Jerome, or just Rome, since at least the age of twelve.

Another cop came in a minute later, shorter, with a pasty, pockmarked face. By their suits and demeanor, I could tell they were big-shot detectives.

"Tell us about March 15th," the shorter one said, sitting down across from me.

The look he gave was so intense I barely registered his words. It wasn't the conqueror's glare, but something more jaded, matter-of-fact. The room seemed to narrow all of a sudden. I could see everything as if it were pressed up against my eyeballs. The anticipation forming through the cop's triangular Slavic skull. His wide right thumb slowly rolling a booger against his finger. The mustard stain on his tie—a bright yellow dot like a tiny headlight shining on me. My hands felt like they'd been stuck in a freezer. I placed them under my thighs, worried the cops would see me shivering.

"It's alright, we got time," the tall one said, taking a seat next to his partner and popping the top on a can of Coke.

I couldn't find my tongue in my mouth.

"March 15th, Jerry," the short one repeated.

It made no sense how they could know.

"Let's start with something simple. Where'd you wake up that morning, Jer?" the tall one asked, sliding the Coke toward me.

The carbonation escaping the can was a hissing snake in my ear.

"Were you at your place or somewhere else?" the short one asked.

I repeated the words *your place* and *somewhere else* in my mind.

"Somewhere else," I said, struggling to get the syllables arranged.

"Was it an apartment or a house?"

I saw it then.

It's just one night, Mom said as she rolled up the window.

"House."

I carried the carnations through the overgrown weeds and up the narrow path to the door.

"Whose house was it, Jerry?"

Harriet acted surprised, though Mom dropped me there every year on the night before her birthday.

"My aunt's."

She was gluing egg cartons to her walls, baseboard to ceiling, to keep out the sound of pigeons shitting under a viaduct a half mile away. She made me help.

"Alright, what'd you do when you got up?"

Cake and coupons, Jerry! Harriet hollered in the morning, handing me a plate of discount bakery gloop, a pair of scissors, and the Sunday inserts. We cut them out and stacked them alphabetically by product—J for Jiffy, K for Kool-Aid—while daytime soaps blared from her console TV and two portable ones.

"Stay with me, Jerry. What'd you do then?"

I was bigger that year. Maybe eleven. Harriet tried putting a greasy brown hair wig on me, same color as hers. I wouldn't let her do it that time. She followed me around her filthy house, saying it louder each time. *Just look in any mirror and you'll see it, sweetie…*

"Jerry?"

I yelled for her to stop, but she wouldn't. I turned with the scissors still in my hand.

"March 15th… *where the fuck were you?*"

She stopped talking so loud then.

Running out the door, I heard, *it's not your fault, son.* I kept running before it became my fault. Mom went to the funeral alone.

A uniformed cop walked in just then.

"Computers back up," he said, glancing toward me and shaking his head at the detectives.

"You gotta be shitting me," the shorter one said.

They held me for a while after the prints came back. I sat alone in that room, staring at the mirror, wondering if anyone was watching from the other side. It must've been midnight by the time they released me. I didn't have enough change to ride the El. It was a long, cold walk home.

The next day, I went out once. Just to get the paper. A headline in the Sun-Times said:

Knic-Knac Nabber Sought in Connection with Homicide

There were a mugshot and a caption underneath: *Ernest Gerard Bardo - aka "Jerry" Bardo*. I recognized him from around the neighborhood. He didn't look that much like me, except for the scar on his forehead. When they caught him, just a few days later, Bardo admitted to the burglaries, but it turned out he wasn't responsible for the murder. I don't know if they ever solved that one.

The only case of mistaken identity I've experienced in all the years since then has been the occasional, "You look like someone I know," from strangers in public places like restaurants or bars. Though I never ask, I sometimes wonder if their friend is Jerry Bardo.

As far as Harriet goes, I can't say if she was my real mom or not. There's no one left in the family to ask about it, either. I'll tell you one thing though, every year the pigeons get a little louder. It's nearly impossible to block them out anymore.

Sponsors

Don Goodrich cleans and shaves the body of his current tenant while the oldies station, KQRS, hums in the background. He begins replacing blood, bile, and urine with embalming solution just as the twelve-string guitar intro to the Eagles' "Hotel California" comes weeping out of his wall-mounted speakers. The oft-repeated recording—itself embalmed and immortalized, spinning incessantly from a DJ-less digital hub somewhere in space—is comforting to Don as it is to the millions of other classic rock connoisseurs who know every verse and movement of the perpetually presented pop relic. Not wanting to foul his stereo with the dead man goo dripping from his rubber-gloved hands, Don reaches his elbow to the volume knob—cranking up the tune while serenading the cleaned-up corpse in an off-key sing-along.

As the song ends, Don turns down the radio and reviews his handiwork. Disturbingly, the tall, white, middle-aged man with receding gray-brown hair laid out on his table looks much like himself. The paunch of front belly, side belly, and gravity-humbled breast blubber hanging on the body cause Don to look down and pinch his own puffy pads.

"Time for group, chubby," he says to the stiff as he grabs his coat and makes his way to the rear exit of Goodrich Mortuary Services.

When he arrives at Pilgrim Lutheran in his shiny 2004 "Eagle Coach" Lincoln hearse, Don checks his watch: 2:45 PM on the dot. He's fifteen minutes early, same as every Saturday. Plenty of time to set up and, most importantly for Don, to claim his special spot in the center of the church basement. After unfolding and lining chairs in perfect rows, Don places a memory foam cushion on the shiniest of the bunch—the chair he disinfects once a week—and sets it in the center of his arrangement. From his Goldilocks position, he greets group members as they slowly filter into the small, wood-paneled room.

Though Don never says much, the fact that he's there holding down the same seat each week has a comforting effect on regulars and newcomers alike. No matter what troubling inconsistencies plague their lives, there's always Don, decked out in beige slacks and blue button-down shirt, offering reassuring nods, waves, and smiles to everyone who enters. He's been coming to the Saturday afternoon gatherings for over twenty years, making Don the longest-standing member, not only of the current recovery group, Overeaters Anonymous, but of every Twelve-Step fellowship that has congregated in Pilgrim Lutheran's basement before them.

When Don first started coming, it was Narcotics Anonymous who held the 3 PM Saturday slot. In those days, Don had been experimenting with "sherm," as embalming fluid-laced cigarettes are known on the street.

"An occupational hazard if ever there was one," he was known to say at meetings.

Don soon found that attending N.A. gave him a sense of purpose and belonging unlike anything he had previously experienced in life. In no time, he'd adopted a slew of Twelve-Step slogans and began using them to great effect during group discussions.

Being a tidy type, Don also took it upon himself to empty the wastebaskets, set up the chairs, and make the coffee.

Group attendees appreciated that Don came early, especially when snacking on the donuts, cookies, and other sweet treats he left near the coffee urn each week. Good old Don. An addict who had really turned his life around. An inspiration to newcomers and old-timers alike.

One Saturday afternoon, two years after Don joined the group, Pilgrim Lutheran's pastor came bursting into the downstairs doper's meeting, demanding that Narcotics Anonymous and its members leave the premises immediately and permanently. The church elders, he said, were fed up with finding hypodermic needles and glassine baggies in Pilgrim Lutheran's bathrooms, pews, and parking lots.

"We have children here. *Children!*" The pastor exclaimed.

As other group members sauntered out of the basement discussing which N.A. meetings they might disperse to, Don, immobilized by the minister's reproachful remarks, clawed his fingers into the folding chair that'd long supported his khaki-covered bottom. The locations his neighbors mentioned moving to sounded so far away. Not just geographically, but emotionally, spiritually.

Though it seemed simple enough for the erratic cohort of intravenous itinerants to jump ship, there was no way Don could abandon his station so easily. That particular spot in that particular basement was where he'd learned to listen to the troubles of others and had, on occasion, even shared a few of his own. It was his place of ease and his place of power. It was the one place in life where the world settled perfectly around him.

And it wasn't just Don who knew it. Other attendees referred to the center seat as "Don's spot" as well. The meeting's secretary had often called on people during the sharing portion of the program in terms of their proximity to the group's most devout member— "Guy next to Don," or "Lady behind Don."

And it wasn't only the people. The fluorescent lights, wood paneling, chipped linoleum, plastic chairs, and coffee machine were also waiting each week for Don to come in, to set up, to take his seat, to bring stability to the space.

The deeper he contemplated the dilemma, the more desperately Don's fingers gripped the seat, as if searching for a hand to hold within its plastic parts. With mind and hands thusly occupied, it was difficult for Don—the room's last holdout—to understand Pilgrim Lutheran's pastor when he said, "I'm talking to *you*, mister," while pointing a stiff arm and long finger toward the exit.

The next Saturday at 2:45 PM, Don returned and waited outside the basement door, hoping the minister and methadoners might reverse course, but sadly it was not to be. When Don went back the following week, there were still no addicts assembled in the church's lower level. But on the third Saturday following the group's demise, Don pulled into Pilgrim Lutheran's backlot to find several smokers standing nonchalantly near the rear entrance. Excitedly, Don strode toward the basement door. There, in its window, he saw a triangular sign advertising an Alcoholics Anonymous meeting. It was scheduled for 3 PM that very day.

Don was more than happy to "keep coming back" as the famous end-of-meeting chant instructed, not at all concerned that the focus of sessions had shifted from drugs to booze. It was no problem for Don to take the first step—admitting his powerlessness over alcohol—when he considered the time he had awoken to find several permanent marker penises scribbled on his skin after a drunken dorm party.

Though the physical and emotional hangovers he'd experienced his first year in college kept him from ever drinking again, after encountering A.A., Don became certain of a latent alcoholic condition residing within himself—ready to take hold if he stopped attending meetings.

As before, Don came early each week to clean up, place chairs, and power the percolator. He studied A.A.'s Big Book rigorously, learning to quote passages and page numbers as well as picking up the proper verbiage for presenting his personal account of living with alcoholism. Other group members appreciated that Don utilized well-worn one-liners during his brief shares, like "put the plug in the jug," "keep an attitude of gratitude," and "I suffer from alcohol*ism*, not alcohol-*wasm*." He was one of the good guys. Someone to look up to. A true recovering alcoholic.

After sixteen years of one drunk helping another, the Saturday afternoon A.A. group—having become quite popular—outgrew the little church basement, necessitating a move to larger locale on the West Side of St. Paul. As previously, Don didn't leave with the others but instead kept his long-settled spot in the center of that particular room in the bowels of that particular building.

And because Pilgrim Lutheran's basement had, by then, become a much sought-after recovery space, it was only one week later that a new Twelve-Step group took over the 3 PM Saturday slot: Gamblers Anonymous.

It was no problem for Don to "qualify" for G.A. when he thought back to his Las Vegas elopement with Dolores—a woman he'd fallen hard and fast for after the two hooked up on his embalming table during a Goodrich funeral service ten years prior.

On the second night of their honeymoon, Dolores came down with a migraine and insisted Don attend the Engelbert Humperdinck show alone.

"Front row seats, Don. You gotta go," she'd said.

Though he preferred not to leave her side, Don did as his bride instructed and caught a cab to Bally's casino. Less than halfway through the performance, however, he thought it best to return to the hotel with two pints of Dolores' favorite ice cream. With the chilly dessert bag in his hand, Don crept quietly into the room. He took a long sneaky inhale and was just about to say "surprise" when he heard grunting. Stepping further in, Don saw a very tan, naked man with a giant pompadour wig doggy-styling his beloved on their honeymoon suite California king. Ketchup-stained food wrappers and bottles of cheap booze littered the giant mattress, framing the corrupt couple like a lurid laurel wreath. Neither Dolores nor the Elvis-impersonating wedding officiant who'd married them the day before heard Don standing near the bathroom muttering "no" under his breath while they did the dirty deed. As his heart sank through his body and fell all of the hotel's thirty-two stories down to ground level, Don, following his vascular organ, slipped from the suite, placed the Ben and Jerry's by the door, and disappeared into the lowest level of the casino. After plonking five hundred dollars' worth of hard-earned quarters into Stardust slots that night, Don caught an early flight back to St. Paul, had a lawyer draw up annulment papers, and swore off relationships for good.

At G.A., no one pried into the details of Don's compulsive gambling. It was enough that they saw the hangdog look on his face when he alluded to the "soul-crushing casino" where he "shook hands with the one-armed bandit." In any event, Pilgrim Lutheran's new anonymous crew didn't last long. With the pass-the-basket money continually disappearing into the pocket of one desperate soul or another, financial instability caused the group to dissolve after just three months.

Two weeks later, in late October of that year, the basement's 3 PM Saturday spot was filled by its first foreign language group: Neuróticos Anónimos.

Great opportunity to practice the old High School Spanish, Don thought, though "Mi nombre es Don y soy neurótico," was the most he felt comfortable saying out loud.

As per usual, Don ingratiated himself by coming early to set up chairs, snacks, and coffee. The small, mostly male congregation welcomed Don warmly, happy to have the gringo mascot in their midst, especially considering what a buena taza de café he made.

Though Don didn't believe himself burdened by neurosis when he first joined the ill-at-ease Latinos, he soon found that he couldn't stop scribbling his name as *Dón* into the many spiral notebooks he'd begun bringing to group. The repeated Dón doodling gave Don a sense of closeness with the others—in both idiosyncrasy and idiom—no matter that it was not the correct Spanish spelling of his name.

The neuróticos meeting, never very large to begin with, began to shrink in numbers as winter set in. Eventually, only two people remained: non-Spanish-speaking Dón and a short, bald man with a robust facial tic named Juan José. Over the span of Neuróticos Anonimos two-man tenure, Don, unable to understand his Hispanic counterpart's hour-long monologues, instead focused on the twitch that zig-zagged from scalp to chin and back again across Juan José's face during the brief moments the Spanish-speaker stopped speaking. The remarkable feat of facial dexterity was an inspiration to Dón who practiced his own eye jerks, nose wiggles, and mouth contortions in the mortuary mirror between meetings each week—sometimes even performing the well-rehearsed facial oscillations for departed souls tabled in Goodrich's lower level.

For Juan José, it had been no problem that the gringo Don was the only other attendee of the recovery sessions, but the lack of proper heating in the church basement was another thing. As brutal January temperatures froze the city of Saint Paul that winter, the group's last Hispanic and his unusual spasm stopped making the chilly trek to Pilgrim Lutheran, leaving Don without a single neurótico to make coffee for.

After Juan José's departure, Don, as he was compelled to do, continued popping around the church each Saturday to check on its Twelve-Step status. Sometimes he even went in, set up a few chairs, and sat alone thinking about his former anonymous allies, wondering where they were and who was making coffee for them.

But as the room remained empty week after week, depression sent Don down a dark path. Though he fantasized about drinking beer, playing the slots, and even smoking a little sherm, Don instead succumbed to what he deemed the least harmful addiction in his repertoire: filling spiral notebooks with *Dóns* while chanting, "Mi nombre es Dón y soy neurótico."

One Saturday at the beginning of spring, as Don and his Dón-filled notebooks drove by Pilgrim Lutheran, he noticed a sandwich sign set outside the church's back door that read: *Overeaters Anonymous today, 3 pm*. Excitedly, he pulled his hearse into the church lot, chuckling to himself about the term *sandwich sign* together with the word *overeater*. Wiping the judgmental joke from his mind, Don stepped out of the car, pulled the band of his beige slacks down a bit, and let his belly protrude.

"Oh yeah," he said, rubbing his newly freed paunch. "You're a natural for this."

The first few weeks in O.A. were a dream. Don memorized the names of regulars and adopted the group's style and vernacular quickly. The overeaters were comforted by their new member's presence and appreciated his setup skills, though they dissuaded him from bringing snacks. More than ever, Don fit right in. And best of all there was no sign of the "Big Bummer."

The thing is, Don was not the only one who kept coming back throughout Pilgrim Lutheran's twenty years of Twelve-Step transitions…

"Name's Ralph an' I'm a *attic*," he introduced himself loudly at his first Narcotics Anonymous meeting.

Don was immediately rankled by the newcomer, who was opposite to himself in every way. Where Don was consistently early, Ralph was always late. Where Don sat in the same spot every session, Ralph moved from place to place—now in the front, now in the back, now standing up, now sitting down—even shifting spots several times during an individual meeting. And where Don, without fail, showed up each week—even if it meant hiring another funeral director to officiate a service—Ralph came and went, sometimes disappearing for a month or more at a time.

While the man's tardiness, lack of commitment, and inability to pick a permanent place had been irksome to Don, Ralph's sloppy clothes, bad personal hygiene, and repeated interruptions of personal shares had been even more irritating. And there were other issues too: Ralph drinking more than his share of the coffee, never contributing when the basket was passed, brazenly flirting with the group's women, and, most painfully for Don, his perpetual misquoting of the renowned end-of-meeting slogan: "Keep coming back, it works *if you're worth it.*"

On top of all that, Ralph exaggeratedly imitated the addictions of whichever Twelve-Step tenant currently occupied the basement, declaring compulsions he seemed to have come down with only upon joining that particular program. In N.A., he presented a rubber-cement-huffing problem. In A.A., he proclaimed his powerlessness over Bailey's "Wild Irish Cream." In G.A., he disclosed an inability to stop dropping dollars at "the bingo." Don, suspecting the Big Bummer of being a big phony, wished the man would leave the recovery room to addicts, like himself, who truly needed it. With the arrival of the neuróticos, Don's wish came true.

"Wonder how you say, '*so long Big Bummer*' in Español," Don laughed, realizing his rival had quit due to a lack of language skills.

The basement remained entirely Ralph-free through the neuróticos run and exactly four weeks into the overeater's takeover. At O.A.'s fifth meeting, however, Ralph reemerged, waving cheerily at Don as he waded through the crowded room well after the session had begun. Don winced, not only because the Bummer was back, but because his nemesis had put on a little weight since last they'd met.

Trying too hard as always, Don thought. *An even bigger bummer than before.*

And so it was, much to Don's displeasure, that Ralph became a semi-regular in the room once again—only this time, Ralph really looked the part.

As he watched Ralph's physical form round out week after week, Don became competitive. But the extra desserts he added here and there weren't enough to keep up with his counterpart. The only way Don could catch up was by doubling portions at every meal…

Three months into O.A. membership, and twenty-five pounds heavier, Don is now more certain than ever that this particular group in this particular place is where he truly belongs. As the last of the overeaters take their seats, Don checks his watch again: 3 PM on the button. He drowsily closes his eyes, hoping the Big Bummer won't show today. But once the sharing portion is underway, Don is awakened by the familiar parlance of his overeating adversary.

"I know whutcher talkin' 'bout, Pam. Them *Dairy Queens* is a big trigger for me too…" Ralph blabs, interrupting the woman next to him.

As Big Bummer's nasal resonations fill the room, Don recalls being cornered at the previous week's meeting.

"Look, I need a sponsor and you're the only guy here wit' real *time* unner his belt. Or over his belt in this case, haha. Look, what I'm sayin' is, I wanna be more like *you*, Don…"

It was horrifying to hear at first, but the more Don thought about it, the more he realized it *would* be good if Ralph were more like him—clean, quiet, punctual—especially considering that the unkempt oaf wasn't likely to leave the Saturday support group anytime soon.

Though he had agreed to take on the role, it wasn't clear to Don which Twelve-Step program he should mentor Ralph in. Never having had a sponsor himself, Don figured the best bet would be to point his pupil toward the proper literature, leaving it to the wisdom of the written word to cure his chaotic counterpart's character defects.

And so it was that Don picked his favorite self-help bookstore, *Endless Evolution*, for their first meeting to take place, setting the date for this Saturday after group.

Meagan Sullivan arrives at *Endless Evolution* to meet her sponsor, Katrina, after their Saturday afternoon Al-Anon meeting. It's a weekly ritual both have come to appreciate over the six months they've been working together. But at a recent Co-Dependents Anonymous session—Meagan's seventh Twelve- Step affiliation since beginning her path to recovery—she was told by long-time group members that having a sponsor is simply "too co-dependent" for someone with problems like hers. Though the words rang true for Meagan, her difficulty with confrontation has kept her from letting go of the many mentors she has in various sex, love, and debt addiction programs. Knowing she'll never rid herself of those relationships until she first fires her closest sponsor, Katrina, Meagan's mind wriggles, searching for the right way to go about it.

As Katrina's yellow VW pulls up, Meagan twists her mouth into an overly excited smile and waves emphatically.

"So, what's happening with Step Four?" Katrina asks, as they stroll toward the bookstore's coffee bar.

"Yeah… I'm still working on it," Meagan says.

"Don't want to get stuck there, girl. Put all those gory details onto paper and let's talk it out. That's when things start to change. You'll see."

"I know…" Meagan says listlessly as she does a quick scan of the room. "There's a couple of books I want to pick up. Meet you up front in a few?"

"That's my girl, always seeking more support," Katrina says, lifting her vanilla latte and gliding toward the newly expanded Incense and Candles section of the store.

"Hey, Don."

"Oh… hi, Ralph," Don says drably, tucking a book entitled *Overcoming Obesity in Obtainable Ways* back on its shelf and checking his watch.

"Sorry, I'm a little late," Ralph says with a shrug.

"You might be interested to know they have an entire section here dedicated to punctuality."

"Had to stop for gas. Then traffic…" Ralph explains.

"As you've likely heard in the rooms, you need a spiritual solution to your malady," Don interrupts, pausing to let the words of wisdom sink in.

Ralph is about to speak when Don starts again,

"This store has many fine selections to help with all sorts of *maladies*. And because your maladies are likely different than mine, you should take a look around and see if there's something suitable for you. I assume you already have the Twelve-Step literature?"

"You bet. And I'm ready to jump in…"

"Whoa… hold your horses. Let's not get ahead of ourselves. How about you figure out your top three or four *maladies* and see if you can find some books here to address them."

Sensing his protégé's hesitation, Don offers another thought.

"Or, you can simply wander the store and see what speaks to you, as I often do."

Don begins a slow stride through the shop with Ralph trailing behind. Passing rows of books on self-improvement, self-empowerment, and self-development, astrology, numerology, and parapsychology, ascended masters, Zen masters, mastering oneself, and meeting one's shadow, Don finally comes to a halt at an endcap rack of half-priced recordings sitting near a CD listening station.

"Oh yes!" Don exclaims, picking out a CD and wagging it at Ralph's eye level. "This is very good. *And well priced.*"

Ralph leans in to read the title:

What Do You Hope To Gain From Your Life? - An audio series by renowned life strategist John Lynwood.

Ralph accepts the item and stares at it blankly.

"And look, it's already in the listening station so you can '*try before you buy*'," Don instructs, pointing at headphones hanging from the CD stand.

As Don follows his malady-mending divination back down book aisles, Ralph turns, bumping into a curvy woman with dyed red hair and cat eye glasses pulling on a pair of headphones at the listening station adjacent to his.

"Hey. Wow. Didn't see you. Maybe I need glasses too, haha…" Ralph says awkwardly.

The woman smiles intensely but doesn't speak. Ralph, unsure of what's happening, smiles back, pulls on a headset, and holds up his John Lynwood CD. The redhead lifts a copy of the same CD and nods in affirmation. They press play simultaneously.

What do you hope to gain from your life? Let's try that again. What-do-you-hope-to-gain-from-your-life? That's the big question, isn't it?

Ralph points at the earphones and smiles playfully at the question. Cat glasses lady responds by pooching her lips and raising her eyebrows along with an 'I dunno' shrug.

To begin with, let's consider each word in the sentence slowly and carefully. 'What' makes it a question. 'Do' makes it an action. 'You,' it's all about your personal journey. 'Hope,' the dreams that are hidden underneath, desperately waiting to be fulfilled…

At the word "hope," the woman nonchalantly undoes the three top buttons on her vintage-style blouse. Ralph's eyes widen.

'To,' a direction or movement forward. 'Gain,' more than there is now.

Playfully undoing a fourth button, the woman looks down at the swelling lump in Ralph's pants.

'From,' the opposite of to—we'll speak more on the power of combining opposites later.

Ralph glances nervously around the room as the woman suddenly seizes his zipper.

'Your,' it inherently belongs to you. 'Life,' something that exists.

Ralph watches speechlessly as she spits in one hand and pulls out his penis with the other.

Altogether, you have a question, an action, a journey, the hidden dreams waiting to become known, the movement that takes one forward, abundance, the power of merging opposites, the inheritance, and finally...the spectacular movement from the energetic realm into full existence.

After a few gentle strokes, Ralph grimaces and stifles a shriek while the henna-haired hottie expertly side-steps the squirting semen emitting from his member.

Now, let's repeat the question. What do you hope to gain from your life? Let this query work its way through your being...

As Ralph finishes zipping his pants, he looks up to see the woman walking away.

"Miss... can I call you?" He asks, dropping the headphones.

"*What you did in there...*" Katrina says, pulling Meagan out of the bookstore.

"I know, I'm *sorry*," Meagan says in a little girl voice.

Just then, two men step out of *Endless Evolution*, interrupting the women's conversation. Meagan pretends not to recognize the one smiling weakly in her direction. As the men turn toward the parking lot, Katrina continues, "There's no point in taking you through the steps if you're just going to *act out* like that!"

After Katrina storms off, Meagan smiles to herself, happy to have taken the first step in working out her co-dependency issues.

Don digs into a double-order fish and chips platter sitting on his embalming table.

"Least it's not burgers," he tells himself.

After the last bite, he washes his hands thoroughly in the slop sink, turns on the oldies station, and pulls on a pair of rubber gloves. As he gets back to work on the body, the strummy guitar intro to the Eagles' *Peaceful Easy Feeling* comes radiating from the radio like sonic sunshine.

"Oh, *yeah*..." Don says, reaching his elbow to the volume knob, feeling how perfectly the middle-of-the-road melody meets his mood.

Don hums along as he matches the cadaver's hair to a mall-style glamor shot lying on its chest.

It's good to be a sponsor, he thinks.

When the song comes to an end, Don turns down the radio and focuses on his last stage of prep.

Wiring the mouth shut and adding caps under the eyelids, he ensures the sensory organs will remain closed from here on in, or at least until the body is deep in the ground.

Self-Help

"You hear that?"

She turned away and pulled the pillow over her head. I tapped. Then I tapped harder.

"What?" she asked too loud.

"I said, *did you hear that*? It sounds like someone talking."

She swatted at me blindly, nearly scratching my eye. I tapped her on the head, which she hates.

"It's probably just the baby," she said.

Our daughter was inches away in the bassinet. I don't know how she thought the low rumble of a grown man's voice in another room was coming from a four-month-old girl lying next to her.

"Where's my cell?" I asked.

"No EMFs in the bedroom."

It bothered me that she'd moved my phone out of the room. It bothered me more that I didn't know what her weird initialism stood for. It's the type of thing my brain chases tirelessly. I ran several possibilities through my mind. One stuck out more than the others: *Esoteric Meat Fragments*. I pictured two cops standing over our dead bodies the next morning—one sipping coffee, the other shaking his head and saying, *They're nothing but esoteric meat fragments now, Frank*.

I thought about escape routes. The most obvious was the bedroom window, but it was blocked.

"We should've taken the air conditioner out," I said.

"We used it just the other night."

"Every year it's the same. Leave it in 'til the frost comes. Now someone's breaking into our house and we're *stuck here*."

I considered nearby weapon-like objects. The stainless-steel water bottle my wife totes everywhere should've been on the nightstand, but for the first time, it wasn't. I'd have to find something else on the way.

"I'm going to look," I told her, hoping she'd stay alert.

"You always do this," she said.

"What are you talking about?"

"You know you do…"

"Would you shut up and *listen?* There's someone *out there*," I whispered hard.

I slipped my feet out from under the covers and stood up. Just then, something fell and thudded on the bedroom floor.

"What was that?"

"Would you *stop?* I have to get up early tomorrow."

"Did you leave your book on the bed again?"

"I don't know, maybe," she said.

"You don't even read them. They're just booby traps."

"Look, if you're going to play intruder alert, get on with it but I have to *sleep*."

"Please keep your *voice down* so I can hear what's going on out there."

Then the baby started whimpering.

"Are you going to get her?" she asked as if that was our biggest worry.

I scooted my toes in front of me until they came to the fallen book. At least it was hardcover. I considered the irony of her unread self-help book saving us from getting chopped into esoteric meat fragments. Then the baby whimpered louder.

"Yes or no?" she asked.

"I have the book…"

"*Oh my god.* You're going to beat a burglar to death with a New York Times bestseller? That ought to make the news."

Her version of irony lacked humor.

"Will you *please stop talking*? He's getting closer..."

She did stop talking then. I guess she heard it too. Even the baby got quieter.

"Are you going to look or not?" she finally asked.

When I heard the fear in her voice, I went from scared to completely terrified.

Since the baby was born, I'd learned all the places to step so the wood wouldn't creak, but my heart was beating so loudly I was sure it could be heard in the next room. When I came to the door, I felt the smooth cool brass of the knob in my hand and wondered if someone was doing the same on the other side. I stood there holding the book over my head, feeling the blood emptying down my arms and into my torso, ready to smash whoever might be there.

As my eyes adjusted to the dark, I could see my wife pulling our daughter into bed and under the covers with her. That was a bad sign. I felt a sudden pang of remorse for all the unkind things I'd said and done in my life, especially to those two.

The sound came again. As I listened closely, it seemed to be emanating from the living room. I got up the nerve and twisted the knob. The door squeaked slightly.

When I reached the hallway, I tipped my head around the corner so I could see the kitchen and the back door. Nothing. I continued toward the front of the house.

Then the baby cried. I hoped the intruder would be scared off—either confronted with a moral dilemma about committing crimes near an infant or worried about a stiffer prison sentence for breaking into a house with one in it—but I didn't hear anyone leave.

When I reached the living room I saw the mess. It looked like a cyclone had hit it. Baby books, clothes, couch cushions, pizza boxes. I moved slowly through the space, waving the book in front of me like a bible in the hand of an exorcizing priest. The front door was locked. The windows were all shut too. But the noise was coming from somewhere nearby. I braced myself.

Out of the corner of my eye, I saw the glowing blue light of the baby monitor on the bookshelf. I didn't remember leaving it on. Moving toward it, I realized the sound was emanating from its fuzzy speaker. I grabbed the little device off the shelf and held it in front of me. What I saw there was confusing. I blinked and looked again. The outline of a dark face began filling the screen. It seemed to be looking back at me too. With the monitor in one trembling hand and the book in the other, I hurried back to the bedroom.

"Did you see anything?" she said.

"Where's the baby cam?" I asked frantically.

She pointed toward the dresser. It was there alright. Aimed at the empty bassinet. I held the monitor near my wife's face.

"I don't see anything," she said.

I looked again. I didn't see anything either. She snatched her book out of my hand and thumped it on the bed in a huff. I went back to the living room and wrote this all down so I wouldn't forget…

My therapist handed me back my notebook and gave me a 'concerned' look.

"Ok. I'm going to stop there Jerry. Let me ask, how did you feel about her taking the book from you?"

"I don't know. Relieved? Angry, maybe? I think you're missing the point though. Did you read it all?"

"I read enough. Here's the thing, I think we'll get to the heart of the matter more effectively if we talk about what's happening in your life rather than you giving me stories to read."

"You said I should journal."

"That's right, but I didn't mean you should bring me your journal… hey… are you writing right *now*?"

"I'm still journaling."

"Well…please listen to me. My take is that you need to work on your relationship with Sheila. I think your writing has become a substitute for genuine connection, perhaps even a competition with the books she's reading. Did you notice that you never once mentioned her name in the story?"

"What about the man's voice and the face in the monitor? I'm pretty sure the house is haunted."

"Ok. Maybe your house *is* haunted, but what if you're being haunted by your disconnection from your wife? It's not uncommon for couples to go through major difficulties when their first child is born."

"You're saying Sheila is the face in the monitor?"

"Jerry, look, our time's about up, so I'm going to give you some homework. I'd like you to pick up a book called *Evolving the Marriage-Friendship*. I think it'll offer some practical advice for your situation…"

"Whoa. EMF. It's Sheila's initialism again."

"See you next week, Jerry. Take good care."

"You shared all that with him?" Sheila asked as she handed my notebook back.

"I'm pretty sure sharing is what people do with a therapist. By the way, it's *she, not he*."

"What? Why didn't you tell me? I mean, I don't care that it's a woman. But you should have told me."

"Yeah, I didn't think you'd care. Anyway, it was your idea for me to see a therapist."

"I'm reading that book, you know."

"Are you *actually* reading it?"

"Do you *honestly* care? You know, you didn't put her name in the story either. Maybe you need to work on your connection with your *female therapist*."

"Oh, that's real good. That's just great. Her name is Sofia, by the way."

"You call her by her first name? Hey… would you please stop writing."

"…but it's getting weirder now, mom. I don't know what you'd call it. I guess he's becoming a compulsive *writer*? Yes, I know Dad was an alcoholic when I was little. Of course, other people have worse problems. Look. Mom. Stop for a minute. Do you want to hear what's going on with me or… OH MY GOD! No, not you. It's *Jerry*. He's been sitting on the other side of the door listening… and writing! I gotta go. What the hell? You cannot eavesdrop on my calls! Stop it. Stop writing!"

Sheila stormed out of the room. For some reason hearing about her alcoholic dad made me thirsty. I walked to the bar.

"Pilsner, please."

"That'll be five."

"I'll have another."

When I finished the second beer, I left a two-dollar tip and went to the men's room.

"You write when you're pissing? Better not be writing about my dick," my urinal neighbor said with zero sarcasm.

"No, I'm just writing what you're saying."

"That's fucked up dude. Stop it."

The guy aimed his phone at me, which, incidentally, he'd been looking at the whole time he was peeing.

"I'm posting this so people know about the creepy shit you do in bathrooms, freak."

"It's called journaling, pal. You might try it sometime."

I tried getting out of there before the confrontation got worse, but I slipped in a puddle of pee. The guy must've thought I was coming at him. He knocked me down. My notebook got wet. My right hand was hurt too.

Sofia handed me back my urine-stained notebook a bit disgustedly, I think.

"Jerry, I'm not reading anymore. We talked about this last week."

We sat silently for a minute or two.

"I used Sheila's name this time."

"Yes, I noticed that. It sounds like you also invaded her privacy as well as the privacy of a stranger in a bathroom. Why do you think you did those things?"

"Now that I think about it, the guy's face looked a lot like the one in the baby monitor."

"Please put the notebook down and look at *me,* Jerry."

"Sorry, I can't use my right hand so well since the whole urinal thing. Give me a minute to catch up…"

"Jerry, I'd like to speak directly to you, not your notebook. Is that possible? Ok… doesn't look like you're stopping. At this point, we need to shift our focus to your writing compulsion. Can you describe for me what it feels like when you write and what it feels like when you don't write?"

"If I stop to think about it, I won't get it all down on the page."

"And what would happen if you didn't get it all down on the page?"

A horrible feeling crept over me when she asked that. I got out of there quick.

Walking through the front door of the office complex, I looked over my last few sentences, making sure I'd written Sofia's exact words. It's so important. I see that now. If I don't get them down just right…

"As I was walking and writing a guy came barreling down the sidewalk. I didn't notice until it was too late. Maybe getting run over by a bicycle doesn't sound like a real thing, but believe me, it is. The guy on the bike was large and heavy. We were both hurt badly. Me worse than him. Oddly, his name

was Edwin Michael Fisher. EMF all over again. And yes, I know now that EMF stands for 'electric and magnetic fields'. It's just weird those letters keep popping up over and over.

The doctors put casts on both of my arms and will soon put screws in one of my hips. Edwin's insurance will cover the bills. I haven't been able to get out of the hospital bed yet. I can't even use my fingers well enough to write.

On the good side, I've started reading that self-help book, *Evolving the Marriage-Friendship*. I'm enjoying it and I really do think it's helping. Truly. I'm not just saying that because Sheila is sitting next to me, writing this all down. Ha ha. You know you don't have to keep writing, honey. We could just spend some time…"

"I just… sorry, I have to go home now."

"Oh. That's too bad. Will I see you tomorrow?"

"I'll call you later."

"Alright, well… give Lisa a kiss from daddy."

I got out of there before he figured it out, though I must admit I don't fully understand myself. After the accident it all happened so quickly. The ambulance driver handing me Jerry's journal. Me reading it, just to make sure he wasn't hiding something. And then, the blank page at the end. Pulling me in. Inviting me to write too…

"986 Laurel Avenue," I said, stepping in the cab.

Mom called again. I know she wants me to come get Lisa. But there's no way. I can't take care of her right now. I can't do anything else right now. The thing is, I know everything will be good again if I can just get the words down properly. They must be organized. They must be complete. They must be perfect…

My God, there's only one page left in Jerry's notebook. There must be a store open.

"Excuse me, sir, I need to stop at the Walgreens…up there on the left."

Mall Doors

Past the first set of automated doors, the cacophony hits me. Past the second set, I'm engulfed. A romantic pop song swelling from a loud but faraway speaker attempts to dominate the space. I don't want to know the lyrics, but I do.

In front of a strong-smelling shop in the first corridor, a smiling lady stands at the ready with lotion sample packets. When someone gets there before me, I pretend search the window display and quickly move on.

A string of repeated words ties up the air nearby. "Today only" is all I make out. Turning the corner, I see a sporty youngster, a full-third too thin for his beige suit waving a clipboard near a sign for discount phone plans. Nano-secondly glimpsing me, he turns to hawk his wares in the opposite direction. I catch my reflection in the window behind him and look away just as quickly.

In the food court, a middle-aged woman extends an impaled meat morsel—smile indicating gift, stance suggesting weapon—as if she'd been waiting for me always. Her oversized, plastic glove brushes my fingers as I accept the challenge. She repeats "tasty" several times in both statement and question form while I chomp the sweet and sour chunk.

"Tasty," I agree, ordering the three-item combo.

Collecting my tray, I mumble "thanks" toward her pivoting face as she baits a toothpick just in time for the next would-be customer. Three inches above my open palm, a young cashier drops change with great precision, the heat of his hand still in the coins.

From the sole empty table, I watch grownups engage children with detached familiarity. It seems the divorce was just yesterday. I tell myself to think "one year" not fourteen months like a baby's age. A few bites into my meal, I rise and dump the tray's contents into an overfull bin, rooting for every rubbery thigh nugget, heat-lamp-hardened noodle, and mushy vegetable to make it through the smudged THANK YOU of the receptacle door, identifying with the ones that don't.

A pot-bellied T-shirt emblazoned with a U.S. map makes me think of routes the U-Haul might've taken. Illinois to Arizona. Five states between no matter which combination of borders they crossed. A completely different place. That's what Lydia said. But the mall, her oasis, is bound to be the same in Scottsdale as it is in Schaumburg.

Map-shirt man sees me staring and shoots a look. I glare back, imagining it's new guy.

Lydia hates driving. New guy probably drove the whole way. I wonder if at any point during the trip, at any lull in the conversation, he considered how many times she and I laughed, fought, ate, stroked each other, and screwed on top of that big leather couch he hauled seventeen hundred miles to palm-tree heaven—a couch we bought at *this* very mall. By now, they've done all the same things on it, left all the same stains. The erection poking at my zipper bothers me more than any of it.

A group of high school girls, maybe college, pass with arms easy around each other, best friends in a hot pink forever. I don't realize I'm following until we near the exit. Their giggles fade with the first set of doors. After the second set, they evaporate completely.

"Fifteen or half hour?" The main concourse masseuse asks.

"Half hour, please," I say, leaning into the face-down chair.

I feel his strong fingers over my shirt; the same one I wore last time. I wonder if he notices.

Another pop anthem streams through mystery speakers. Lydia's music. I bring it close this time, cranking the bass and drums from within. It doesn't mask everything, but if I concentrate hard enough, it covers the automated hum running through this place, running through all of us.

Existing Nail Feng Shui

"The place looks great, but the sign out front. I didn't see a price…"

"For you two? I can go nine hundred," Otto, the building's owner, says.

The couple, Sabrina and Denis, fall silent, exchange glances.

Overdressed for the late June weather, Otto unfastens the top button of his sports jacket and removes a document from its inner pocket.

"I know. It's less than other rentals in the area. But you two seem great, and I don't believe in overcharging. There's one important stipulation," he adds, reaching the lease toward the would-be renters.

"Wow, exactly in our budget," Denis says, snatching the papers excitedly.

"What's the stipulation?" Sabrina asks cautiously, folding her delicate brown arms below V-neck T-shirt cleavage.

"You'll notice there are two nails in each room for you to hang pictures, mirrors, whatever you like. They are not to be removed, and you are not to add new nails. Think of it as *existing nail Feng Shui*," Otto says, chuckling halfheartedly. "If that works for you, we can discuss security deposit and so on…"

Twenty minutes later, at a faux diner called The Hungry Hen, the couple lob words over large plastic menus.

"Didn't that existing nail thing seem strange?" Sabrina asks.

"The Feng Shui part made me want Chinese instead of overpriced sandwiches," Denis says.

"Did you see his eyes when he said it?"

"He was wearing tinted glasses."

"Whatever, his face was serious. It was a very serious statement."

"The guy doesn't wanna damage the walls. Like any landlord."

As the waitress approaches, Sabrina drops the menu and plucks the lease from her purse.

"Look, he actually wrote it in there. It's under *Grounds for Tenant Removal*," she says, exhibiting the offensive paragraph.

"A place that size, in this neighborhood? Anyway, we gave him the check, Breen. It's done."

Sabrina's fifty-five-year-old dad, Ed, moves the last of the load toward the U-Haul's ramp. Just twelve years older than Denis and similarly built—medium tall with twice-a-week gym muscles—he handily heaves a familiar box onto his shoulder. With the weight of his daughter's bad choices on his worn rotator cuff, Ed climbs the three-flat brownstone's stairs two at a time, hoping the new guy will work out.

"Where you want the paintings, Breen?" he yells into the tall-ceilinged entryway of the two-bedroom apartment.

"Let's take 'em to the storage room," Denis directs quietly.

Before Ed reaches the back door, Sabrina emerges from the pantry, stopping him.

"Uh uh. Those go in the main room," she redirects.

As Sabrina unpacks a canvas from the large box, Denis pretend-arranges a small table and lamp in a corner. They'd already agreed, more or less, that the living room's existing nails were too oddly placed—one too high, one too low—to hang her artwork. A relief for Denis, because no matter how much he tries, he can't get his head around Sabrina's weird collages, every one of which is formed out of feminine product scraps. Tampons, vaginal cream tubes, cutouts from women's magazines, panties, makeup smears. It isn't the symbolism, the feminine thing, that bothers him, but the random arrangement of said implements. Like she'd dumped the contents of a ladies' room trash bin onto a big, gluey surface. It was no prob when they had separate places, but these walls are his too.

Of Denis's past girlfriends—most of them artists, and all, like Sabrina, whom he met through bartending—there was only one other he lived with. A self-styled poetess, Delilah, lasted just one go round on a twelve-month lease before the trouble set in—the trouble being her depression, or so Denis informed his circle of bar bros and gym dudes afterward.

Though he didn't much care for Delilah's writing—multisyllabic rigamaroles full of vague symbolism that came peeping out of her like melancholic Morse code—Denis made appearances at her poetry readings, applauded at appropriate times, and congratulated her at the end of said presentations. But that was different. That was okay. For one thing, the readings were held in trendy cafes or hipster dives like The Lion's Den—the bar he tended, still tends—well outside the safety zone of their apartment. True, Delilah spent a lot of time scribbling her mumbo jumbo at home. But he didn't have to listen to the readings in their living room. Or worse, look at it on the wall…

The longer he stares at Sabrina's picture, the less he understands what the hell he's supposed to be looking at. Every item and image on the canvas is a wrong way rub for Denis. Like the zesting side of a cheese grater, scraping eyeballs and nutsack simultaneously.

A phrase his mother used pops into his head just now: "Art is meant to make you *feel*."

Oh, I feel something alright.

More than anything, it's the niggling insecurity. The suspicion that Sabrina has access to things he doesn't. Abstract things. Artistic things. Entire worlds he's not privy to.

"Help me with this, will you?" Sabrina asks, reaching her gaudiest amalgamation—a piece called *Leftover Lavender* or *Lavender Leftovers*, he's never been sure which—toward the higher of the living room's two nails.

Denis takes charge, hoping to show how ridiculous the collage will look that far up the wall. Once it's hooked, he steps back, narrowing his eyes. Sabrina's mashup, he decides, makes his mother's art seem uncomplicated by comparison.

On the few and far between occasions when Alice, his mother, came to visit, it invariably meant a trip to a gallery or coffee shop. Some little place where her smudgy watercolors hung with titles, prices, and her artist name, *Allegra*, printed just below. At ages five, eight, and ten, young Denis feigned delight in his mother's "work," though the images made about as much sense as how they came to be hanging on walls in San Diego when she lived, according to his grandparents, a long plane ride away in a city whose name was ever-changing.

"Why do they call it *Chicago* now?" He'd asked once.

"You're lucky Chula Vista's still Chula Vista," his Grandpa had said.

Ed lumbers into the living room just now, loaded with more boxes, his T-shirt and shorts soaked with vinegary sweat.

"Dad, what do you think?" Sabrina asks, motioning toward the twenty-four by thirty-six canvas covered in toiletries, unmentionables, clippings, glitter.

"Yeah, well. If that's where you want it…"

"We talked about this, Sugar. The nail's too high. It's practically on the ceiling," Denis interjects.

"Hell, let's just add a new one," Ed says, rapping a meaty fist against the wall, searching out a solid nail-sinking spot.

"Actually, there's a stipulation in the lease…" Denis starts.

Sabrina stomps down the hall, slamming a door behind her. Pillow-muffled wails follow.

"Got anything to drink?" Ed shrugs.

Denis finds his liquor supply buried, intentionally, he thinks, under a pyramid of boxes in a corner of the pantry.

With a fifth of Wild Turkey and two ice-filled tumblers, the men descend the stairwell and settle on the cement stoop out front. Sipping the booze not-so-slowly, they set their gaze upon the empty U-Haul's blinking hazards.

From their newly purchased California King, Sabrina stares at a duo of leftover nails protruding from the bedroom wall. As with the living room nails, they're too peculiarly positioned to hang anything properly.

That one's Denis. That one's Dad.

When Sabrina first introduced them, it was a relief to discover they had something in common. Even if it was just a shared love of hard liquor. But the bond she'd hoped for, one based on a mutual appreciation of who she is and what she wants to be in this world, that one never came. And it never will come, she sees now, because Denis and Dad have never been supportive. Neither has ever been a proper nail lodged in a proper place. A nail whose purpose is to hold Sabrina up in the bright, eye-level space of a main room where she can be witnessed, understood, appreciated.

Hearing the U-Haul's roll-up door clang shut, Sabrina rises slowly, knowing it'll take Denis a half hour or more to drop off her dad and the truck.

In the apartment's second bedroom, which they'd agreed would be her office, she unpacks art implements and feminine products, arranging them in desk drawers. Thumbing through a stack of old magazines—*Mademoiselle, Ebony, Vanity Fair*—her mind skips around textures, shapes, colors, words—a playful place where the creative possibilities are endless.

Denis awakens late and hungover. He flops a lazy hand to the bed's center, then further over, searching for the warmth and density of human flesh. Nothing but pillows. A lot of them. Tossing feet overboard, Denis arranges his posture on unsteady legs and maneuvers through an obstacle course of unpacked boxes. Moving stealthily from room to room, he tightens his peripheral vision, keeping the mess at bay. More than anything, trying to keep last night's fight at bay. But the tighter he squints, the more clearly the argument replays in his mind.

"They can't stay like that," he'd said, waving drunkenly at the many canvases propped on bookshelves and end tables.

"Til you figure out the nail problem, that's exactly where they'll stay."

"Why're you putting this on me?"

"Because you're the one who stuck us in this *trap*!"

"Christ. I found a great place. One we can afford. Isn't that more important than hanging *collages*?"

"Go ahead. Say it,"

"Come on, Breen,"

"Just say it."

"Fine. They can stay where they are."

"If you hate them so much, if you hate what I do, why do you want to *live* with me?" She had shouted as he neared the kitchen and the near-empty bottle.

"I don't hate 'em, Breen. But it's like… we have to share this space. You know?"

"And I have to listen to your music. You think I like hearing *The Rockford Files* on repeat?"

"I don't play it on repeat."

"You play it every single fucking day."

The thing is, for Denis, *The Rockford Files* theme is more than a song. It's a nerve-settling tonic. Musical medicine. The 70s-era detective drama was Mac and Dottie's, his grandparents', favorite show. Denis grew to love it too, though for him it was as much about the hour of day the show aired—3 PM—than anything. By that time, his elderly caregivers had, generally speaking, consumed no more than two tumblers of watered-down bourbon each. A light greasing of the wheels before rerun fun.

"Rockford's on!" Dottie would call spiritedly at three on the dot.

As ever, Denis would be hiding around a corner, anxiously waiting for the theme to start, his inner clock set precisely to Rockford time. Then, entering the small living room where everything and everyone was aimed at the large RCA console television, Denis would take his place mid-couch in front of a Salisbury Steak frozen dinner or some similar rectangle-meat TV tray meal. During the show's seventy-second opening sequence, Denis reveled in the familiar images, soundtrack, and emotional climate as James Garner and Jim Beam brought love and light after passive-aggressive mornings and manipulative middays. Of course, later, as the bottle drained more quickly, the old folks' equilibrium tipped to a darker place. But from three to four, young Denis was a welcome addition to the household. An asset even. Because for that one hour, with faultless timing and incredible skill of memory, Denis preemptively cracked every smart-ass one-liner a moment before it quipped from Rockford's strong-chinned mug, mimicking the leading man with his best ten-year-old tough guy groan.

"By god, the boy knows 'em all," Mac would cheer, lifting his glass for Denis to refill.

But the punchlines weren't all the boy retained of the reruns. Before he was big enough to buy a 45 RPM single of the song, Denis had memorized every note of the whiny synthesizer, campfire harmonica, wailing guitar, and orchestral arrangement that composed Rockford's opening music. And there, in his troubled mind, he did play the song on repeat. Every time his emotional landscape threatened to overtake him, as it did arguing with Sabrina last night, Denis's subconscious cranked up Rockford, narrowing his experience, settling his nerves.

Now, stumbling into the kitchen and switching on the coffee machine, Denis considers how he wound up in this mess to begin with. How six months ago, Sabrina showed up at The Lion's Den Christmas party. How she and her friends took turns flirting with him. How she started popping around during his shifts, setting the bait, reeling him in. The most beautiful, confident, and well-dressed woman in the bar, always.

"I can't keep this up from separate apartments," she'd said after their first weekend trip.

Maybe he gave in too soon. But with her cutting him off sex for a month. And then his lease ending on the studio apartment. Not to mention what a pain in the ass it'd become juggling bar chicks. Anyway, he's not so young anymore. What was he going to do, spend the rest of his life living in a fourteen-by-eighteen-foot room around the corner from The Lion's Den?

Sabrina comes in quietly and reaches her arms around his waist.

"I don't want to fight anymore," she says.

"Same here," Denis says.

"Oh, Honey, I love you! Did you see where I set *Lavender Leviathan*? I know, it's where we wanted the TV, but it's so perfect there. Dad left some more nails…"

With a guitar solo wailing behind his forehead, Denis squeezes a Rockford grin onto his face. The one Sabrina loves so much. The one everybody loves so much.

Mashed Potato Time

On October 21st, 1962, Hurley Brennan climbed behind the wheel of his Chevy Apache and headed to Pocatello on errands. When he could no longer see his farm in the rearview, he flipped on the radio, for it was Hurley's secret pleasure to tune in pop music shows broadcasting out of Idaho Falls or Salt Lake City when he was alone. And alone he was on that day, in that truck, when he first heard Dee Dee Sharp describing in verse a dance named after the foodstuff that was the primary source of his financial and dietary sustenance. The bouncy bubblegum ditty was instantly familiar to the farmer as it shared the same melody, four/four drum pattern, and high backing *wha-oo's* as The Marvelettes' 1961 hit "Please Mr. Postman." But it was the theme of the new song, the potatoes, that drew him in.

In church, he'd been told repeatedly, as the whole congregation had, that rhythm & blues and rock 'n' roll were the Devil's music, that where they took hold of an ear they'd snatch a soul. Hurley rationalized his indulgence in the dubious entertainment with the excuse that he needed to "know the enemy's tactics," as Bishop Taylor had often preached. But driving to Pocatello that morning, Hurley had a hard time believing that Dee Dee Sharp, a woman singing a peppy song about mashed potatoes, was his adversary.

It seemed an odd coincidence to Hurley that "Mashed Potato Time" was also playing on the RCA color televisions in Block's display window as he walked toward the department store's entrance. Hurley looked both ways, lest there be any fellow parishioners around, before ogling the scantily clad women doing the Mashed Potato dance on *American Bandstand*.

After buying needed items at Block's and running a few more errands around town, Hurley made his way home, purposefully leaving the radio off—as he did most return trips—to offset his earlier intemperance and leave room for the Lord to speak should He desire to do so. Though he waited patiently for a message from above during the hour-long voyage, all Hurley heard was Dee Dee as if her voice were still crackling through the truck's single speaker.

It was a joy to pull up to the farm at the close of a sunny afternoon and find his two daughters playing in the yard while his wife, Margaret, hung clothes on a line between their home and a river birch tree. Hurley stepped out of the truck and gathered the boxes and bags from Block's. Debbie, his youngest, scrambled toward him, flashing a smile devoid of front teeth.

"What'd you get me, Papa?"

"Something to keep you warm this winter."

"Is it pwetty?"

"Not too pretty."

Debbie made a pouty face and went back to playing with her older sister, Clara.

Hurley, with all five of his sense organs and his thinking mind too, took in the thirty-seven-acre potato farm stretched out before him, relieved for the end of harvest season and happy for the extra income the seven new acres had brought in. Walking toward the front door with an armload of purchases, he stopped to watch Clara dancing a large potato dressed in raggedy doll clothes with Debbie's Barbie.

"Been digging your own harvest?" Hurley asked.

Clara smiled and held up her dolly. "Look at my *tater lady*, Papa," she said proudly.

It happened now and again that potatoes grew fissures, deformed and knobby, that resembled body parts. It wasn't altogether uncommon to find one that had grown "arms" or "legs." Some even appeared to have heads with faces. But the potato Clara held up not only had a head and four stubby appendages, it had something else, too.

Hurley set down the packages and took the curious doll in his meaty hands. He couldn't understand it. Not just how human the potato looked, but how *feminine*.

At first, Hurley thought, the two bumps under the doll's blouse must have been added by Clara, who was herself just beginning to form chest bumps. But upon lifting the homemade blouse, Hurley was shocked to discover the two round shapes were inseparable from the peculiar potato.

"Stop, Papa, we're pwaying wif her," Debbie cried as Hurley shambled toward the house, stripping off the doll's clothes.

"No, Papa! Bring her back! Please…" Clara called.

Staring at the deformed tuber, Hurley walked trance-like through the doorway and collapsed onto the sofa. He blinked his eyes, shook his head, and looked again. What he witnessed upon removal of the doll's skirt was stranger, even more improbable than the rest. There, between the humanlike potato's stubby legs, were detailed outlines of a labia. And when Hurley squinted and looked even closer, he spied the legendary "little man in the canoe," as his high school classmates had called the pleasure button that sat atop a woman's private parts. Invasive images of past lustful deeds suddenly took over Hurley's mind, adding more confusion to the moment.

Seized with a sudden dread, Hurley moved swiftly to the kitchen and grabbed a butcher knife. The girls came in crying just then, shivering as they watched their father, with red face and twisted brow, chopping their dolly to pieces.

"Where'd you girls find this…*thing*?" Hurley yelled, staring nervously at the decimated potato, as though its parts might grow back together at any moment.

When they didn't respond, Hurley grabbed the girls by the arms and made them walk him to the place—one of the new fields far out back of the house—where they'd discovered the potato lady.

The hole the girls showed their father was at least three feet in diameter and as many feet deep. It seemed to Hurley too large a pit to have been dug by his daughters, but before he could ask if it was their doing, they had run away.

Over the next hours, Hurley shoveled the hole deeper and wider, occasionally finding other odd-shaped potatoes. Some were quite large and buried at unusual depths. None were human in shape, but they weren't the normal kind either. After scrutinizing each one for feminine features, Hurley tossed them over his shoulder and kept shoveling.

"I'll dig clear to Satan's cupboard if I haffta!" he thundered.

As the sun was setting, Margaret swung the front porch dinner bell until its yoke nearly gave way. The girls, who'd been hiding since the destruction of their dolly, eventually answered the call and pointed dirty fingers in the direction of their daddy. Margaret marched that way until she saw dirt and potatoes flinging above the flat earth.

"Supper's on, Papa. Best come while it's warm," Margaret hollered toward the hole without question or concern for Hurley's doings.

After his wife's words hit the hole, Hurley lifted his chin toward the darkening sky, waiting for the Lord to speak. A long minute later, with no words from above, Hurley scrambled out of the pit, suddenly afraid he might fall through the earth at any moment.

The family was sitting quietly at the table when Hurley arrived. The girls stared at the floor, breathing uneasily. Following Margaret's lead, they joined hands with Hurley as he took his seat, their fingers fidgeting in his tight grip.

"Dear Lord, our Father, we thank you for the bounty you have given us. We ask you to forgive our indulgences. To watch over and keep us in your grace. To bless this house and this family…"

Margaret, thinking Hurley was about at the amen part, began to let the girls' hands slip from her own, but when she saw her husband's tight, twitching eyelids, she realized he was meaning to say more. And more he did say.

"Father… please don't forsake us! If these *are* the last days, show us how to follow the path to your Kingdom."

Hurley looked up, as if from a bad dream, and stared blankly ahead. Moving on from the moment, Margaret began placing meatloaf, mashed potatoes, and green beans on the girls' plates.

"You stop at the bank, Hurl?"

"Yeah."

"What'd they say 'bout the car loan?"

"We have plenty collateral."

Hurley dropped his gaze to his food-piled plate. A few bites later, he scooched his chair from the table and left the house without a word. As he walked under the waning moon, memories, like city traffic, came and went, crowding his head 'til it hurt.

"That's when people still believed, Lord," Hurley said to the sky.

They were just cartoons that played when he was sleeping. Bad cartoons. Hadn't occurred to him to say anything to anyone. Wasn't 'til he caught a whooping for bedwetting that Hurley told what he'd been seeing, what showed itself to him some nights. When they found out about it, three of the elders—ones who still put faith in apocalyptic prophecy—took turns listening, writing down details, and encouraging the boy to testify at service. Some church folk said he was "anointed," others said he was "touched." Young Hurley could barely pronounce pock-a-lips, judge-men day was easier.

As Hurley came of age, and as his visions became increasingly strange, and as the older, true-believing elders were no longer living or no longer willing to share in his enthusiasm for the end times, Hurley found himself increasingly isolated with the scenes that played out in his mind. Parents, elders, and other parishioners nearly convinced him they were just nightmares, imagination run wild. But the last one— "the incident" as they later called it—had come to him so clear. It was as if someone had suddenly parted curtains or wiped smudge off a dirty window.

Halloween, 1952. Hurley, having come straight from the fields, walked into the school gymnasium wearing jeans and flannel. Though his hardline Mormon parents didn't permit him to celebrate the ghoulish holiday, he went to the party anyway, hoping to see girls in skimpy getups, wanting to be part of something other than farm work, church, and studies. The other high school seniors dressed as vampires, Frankensteins, ghosts, and zombies, made fun of their un-costumed classmate. Hurley was used to being the butt of jokes, but this time something was different.

It was the odd way of talking that first caught his attention. Hurley thought it was a gag, an inside joke, until the kids started bickering with one another—snippy remarks that became nasty comments that became the worst kind of cussing. The type of things that, if said at all, could only be said in private, behind someone's back. As the exchanges grew more heated, Hurley noticed how tortured, how desperate the whole thing was, as if his classmates, for the sake of their own survival, *had* to emit such blasphemous phrases.

And then, one by one, they began taking off their masks. It was almost funny how caricature-like they looked underneath, as if the worst trait, the most negative part of each personality, had risen to the surface, projecting right through their noses, mouths, eyes…

It was the music, Hurley thought, the Devil's music that was activating their bad behavior. The rhythm & blues kept slowing down and speeding up until it was hard to tell what the song even was anymore. The high schoolers twitched and contorted to it—hunching, snarling, writhing in circles—waiting for a signal, Hurley thought, that would come any moment. A signal for them to stop pretending to be people.

As he bounded from the gym and away from the school, Hurley saw a huge explosion in the sky. He ran clear to Elder Baumgarten's house, demanding the elder call the Bishop. Though they listened to the rantings with measured patience, neither the Bishop nor the Elder could calm the hysterical boy. They told him repeatedly that he'd only been daydreaming, that if it'd been a true prophetic vision, he would've seen signs and symbols, the appearance of ancient figures, the righteous vindicated and the opposition vanquished, and, most importantly, he would've seen Jesus making his triumphant return.

It wasn't until two years later that news of "Operation Ivy," the first testing of a hydrogen bomb by the United States government, was acknowledged to have been conducted on Nov 1st, 1952—the day after Hurley's vision. The 82-ton bomb detonated that day was said to have been 500 times more powerful than the deadly atomic bomb dropped on Nagasaki. Its blast vaporized an entire island in the Western Pacific, leaving in its place a fifteen-story crater more than a mile in diameter. Though Hurley initially thought himself vindicated by the news, he soon found that people had lost interest in "the incident." From that point forward, Hurley realized, there was no one he could rely on but God Himself.

As he grew tired of pacing the fields, Hurley returned home, climbed into bed with Margaret, and closed his eyes. Best not to mention the girls' potato, he thought. Throughout the night, along with his fitful sleep, dreams came as if broadcast through an RCA color television. He tried changing channels, but every station played the same show: *American Bandstand*. On the TV, he saw himself, his family, and a group of brown-skinned people dressed in ancient robes dancing the Mashed Potato to a performance by Dee Dee Sharp. As the music played, as the people danced, cameras occasionally panned the TV studio's windows. Outside and all around the building, Hurley glimpsed nuclear blasts vaporizing the planet.

When Hurley awoke the next morning, October 22nd, 1962, the intense dream was still playing in his mind. And unlike previous visions, Hurley thought, this one had all the characteristics of a true prophecy. Signs, symbols, ancient figures—even the return of Jesus Christ.

Margaret was already sitting up at the time Hurley arose. When she saw his gray-blue eyes peek out from under the lids, she started crying.

"Jesus is coming," she said gently, wiping tears and laughing.

The couple held each other close, laughing and crying with joy. For not only had they both seen Jesus in their dreams, they'd both seen the same *kind* of Jesus. And, strangely, the dream-Savior they both described, the one they both knew to be Jesus, was not white. And not only was He not white, but He was not a "he" at all. The Christ in their dreams, the One they both bore witness to, was a Black woman.

Hearing the commotion, Clara and Debbie had awoken as well. They cracked the door to their parents' bedroom tentatively. Hurley waved them over and patted the bed.

When the girls climbed in, Hurley asked excitedly, "Did you see it too?"

Clara and Debbie looked to their mother's soft, smiling face and then nodded.

After several joyful and affectionate minutes together, Margaret went to the kitchen to cook breakfast. Hurley, dancing throughout the house with the girls, took in a whiff of the delicious food and suddenly understood what had happened.

"It's the *tater!*" he shouted.

It was as clear as the big blue sky. "Mashed Potato Time" meant the apocalypse, Judgment Day. That was the message from God's dark-skinned Daughter, Dee Dee. The potato lady his girls had discovered was none other than the holy sacrament, the body of Christ. Margaret must've cooked its butchered pieces along with the other spuds.

Hurley raised the steaming pot of mashed potato leftovers above his head, realizing that the chosen ones, the true Latter-day Saints who would join Dee Dee Christ in the Mashed Potato Time, must first partake of the sacred spud as he and his family had done.

Frantically, Hurley called his church friends, recounting the vision, the potato doll, the second coming. Few listened more than a minute.

With the pot of leftovers by his side, Hurley jumped in the Chevy and drove straight to Bishop Taylor's house in Pocatello. Interrupted from his breakfast, the Bishop answered the door and hesitatingly invited the young man in. He bit his tongue while Hurley rattled on about a radio song, a female-shaped potato, and ancient figures dancing on TV. He remembered well the boy's apocalyptic rantings from years before but had hoped he would've outgrown such nonsense. When Hurley got to the part about a dark-skinned She-Jesus, the Bishop could take no more.

"*Now you listen to me*, son. A true prophet, Nephi, once said, 'Satan seeketh that all men might be miserable like unto himself,' and you, my boy, are looking *mighty* miserable right now."

The Bishop went on to tell Hurley about the dangers of demon-led visions. Further saying that Satan was using Black people to destroy the agency of God's children, enticing them with rock 'n' roll and lewd dancing.

When Hurley saw there was little hope of convincing the church leader, he dabbed a spoonful of spuds on a tea saucer in case the unbelieving Bishop later changed his mind. From there, Hurley stopped at Brock's Department Store, where he purchased a portable record player and a 45 RPM single of Dee Dee Sharp's "Mashed Potato Time." On the drive home, Hurley flipped on the radio, for unlike Bishop Taylor, he now knew that the Lord spoke through Black rock 'n' roll singers.

That evening, while Hurley and his family danced the Mashed Potato, waiting for Lady Jesus to carry them home, John F. Kennedy gave a television address from the Oval Office of the "highest national urgency." The president revealed to the American people evidence of Russian nuclear missiles in Cuba and spoke of how far the missiles could travel—all the way to Washington D.C.

Several fellow parishioners who watched the president's frightening speech that evening, and who pieced it together with Hurley's prophetic phone call, went immediately to the Brennan home seeking help. The dozen or so church folk who showed up at his door were welcomed inside and invited to partake in mashed potatoes—both the food and the dance—while they awaited the Judgment.

In the days that followed, with the world still standing—and no sign of Jesus—word got around about the "rock 'n roll orgy" that had occurred at the Brennan place. In response, Elder Baumgarten, other elders, counselors, and even some who ate and danced that night in Hurley's home, demanded the Brennans be excommunicated from the Mormon faith.

A disciplinary council came to order soon thereafter. When Hurley would neither denounce his visions nor his actions, he and his family were disfellowshipped and told never to darken the doors of a Mormon temple again. Bishop Taylor was the only high-ranking member who did not vote to expel the "false prophet."

Unwilling to remain in the hostile environment, Hurley found a buyer for the farm. Loading his family and needed possessions into the pickup, he began driving south toward Mexico, where he'd heard other Latter-day Saints, outcasts like himself, had made a home. There, in the Sierra Madre Mountains among other exiles, Hurley testified and bore witness once again. Though the Mormon transplants appreciated his fervor for the final days, none welcomed talk of a Black Lady Jesus or believed it appropriate to use pop music for prophetic practice. Hurley, noticing that many in the group were engaged in polygamy, didn't feel comfortable with them either.

Outcasts once again, the Brennans left the American Mormon enclave with no direction and, even more devastating for Margaret, no church affiliation.

Piling his family back into the pickup, Hurley flipped on the radio, hoping to hear the Lord speak through one of his rock 'n' roll messengers once again. But as they traveled deeper into Mexico, and farther from the "border blaster" stations that played American music, they found themselves completely immersed in Spanish-language programming.

As the days went on and they traveled further south, Margaret worried openly about the girls' lack of home, school, and church. Hurley, who'd continued to dream of the dark female Christ, and who was certain they were getting closer to Her, encouraged his wife to hang on while sharing details of his visions.

"She comes to me every night, darling. Speaking Spanish now. Spanish!"

When they stopped in villages for food, toilets, and gas, Hurley had his daughters, who'd been quick to pick up Spanish words and phrases, ask the locals about a Black woman Savior. They had little luck the first few days, but one afternoon, at a roadside lunch stand, a stocky woman making tortillas nodded affirmatively at the girls' query. Flashing a gold-toothed smile, the woman spoke to the Brennans of La Morenita, The Dear Dark One. When Hurley, excitedly, asked where they could find Her, the woman replied mysteriously that the Santa Madre, La Morenita, was *everywhere*.

With a renewed sense of purpose, the Brennans continued their journey south, asking about The Dear Dark One at every opportunity. Several villagers they met along the way told them of a place called Tepeyac, a hillside north of Mexico City, where La Morenita was known to appear.

When the Americans arrived at Tepeyac, they were welcomed by other pilgrims on their way to visit La Morenita at her home, the Basilica of Guadalupe. There, both inside and outside the cathedral, the Brennans found many devotees praying to a dark-skinned Virgin Mary. Among the faithful rubbing rosaries, offering candlelight, and kneeling in prayer, the family met some who claimed that Santa Maria, La Morenita, was more than just the mother of Jesus, as the *Católicos* believed. One such devotee, an old man named Don Pepe, put it to them this way,

"How can She be the mother of God, and not be the mother of *Everything*?"

When Hurley and Margaret indicated they were eager to hear more, Don Pepe invited them to join his camp nearby. As the Americans approached, several copper-skinned people who sat gazing into a fire acknowledged the newcomers with a simple nod of the head. Hurley waited some minutes, and when no one spoke, he jumped headlong into a description of his visions. Clara and Debbie kept up with their father best they could, interpreting with gestures and broken Spanish, though it wasn't clear what, if anything, was getting through.

At the conclusion of Hurley's monologue, the campers talked quietly among themselves in a language unrecognizable to the Brennan girls or their parents. After several minutes, Don Pepe turned his attention back to the Americans. Speaking slowly in Spanish, he explained that there are people in his own village, people like Hurley, who dance, sing, and eat sacred plants to bring visions. These people, he said, are called *curanderos*.

Don Pepe's wife, known to others in the camp as Abuelita, called the Brennan girls to her. She played a game with them, something like patty-cake, then guided them to touch various rocks and plants nearby. When they were finished playing, Abuelita announced, matter-of-factly, that the girls had special gifts and that she would like to train them. After camping two more days with Don Pepe and Abuelita, the decision was made.

The Brennans followed their new friends to Huautla de Jiménez in the northern corner of Oaxaca. Abuelita and Don Pepe helped the Americans settle in with Los Mazatecos, as the people in the community called themselves. Hurley joined in with the farmers while Margaret shared in the many tasks of housekeeping. The girls were enrolled in the local school but took their real education from Abuelita.

As Los Mazatecos shared their ways with the Americans, the Brennans, in turn, offered a few of their own. The Mashed Potato dance in particular was an instant hit. It was not long before "Baile de Papas" blended in with other ritual dances, becoming part of the local harvest ceremony.

Margaret, over time, found a place for herself as a teacher of English and mathematics at the local school. Clara and Debbie, after receiving full initiation into the Mazatec tradition, became sought-after healers in their own right. Hurley, who occasionally ate sacred plants with the Mazatec curanderos and curanderas, continued to have visions for the duration of his life, though he stopped speaking of "the last days" until his own last day, when, on his deathbed, he called out to Margaret, "It's Mashed Potato Time."

A few old-timers in southeastern Idaho still remember the Brennan place and what happened there on October 22nd, 1962. No one has dug up a potato lady since the Brennans left.

Closer

In fifth grade, I was obsessed with Jocelyn Ramirez. I swooned over her soft, round face, bubbly voice, long dark ponytail, and slender fingers that drew beautiful cursive words. At my desk each day, I'd spell out her name in block letters, crisscrossing my own name, Ryan Tierney, into it as the header for the "I like you" notes I took great care to write, but inevitably ripped up and dropped in the trash.

Like most kids at school, Jocelyn didn't seem to notice me. But one particularly sunny December morning at recess, she acknowledged my existence with one simple sentence:

"Hey, *you*! I dare you to step on this crack."

I stood frozen, taking in the situation. It seemed Jocelyn and her friends were playing *dare*—like "truth or dare" without the truth. I didn't know if they were inviting me to join them or setting me up as the butt of a joke. No matter the case, answering the call of my dream girl was a choiceless move.

With the group eyeballing me, I strode over as nonchalantly as possible and placed the toe of my right no-name sneaker on the crack.

"That's not enough," a boy behind Jocelyn shouted.

I hadn't developed many superstitious beliefs up to that point in my life, or wasn't aware if I had, but with the kids making such a big deal of the dare, I began to feel self-conscious. Slowly, deliberately, I raised my foot above the crack and stepped on it.

"Still not enough. You gotta jump on it with both feet!" I heard someone say.

I searched Jocelyn's face and saw her eagerness for me to fulfill the command. Dramatically, I placed my feet just behind the crack—like an athlete at the starting line—and crouched down. I jumped as high as I could, maybe a foot in the air, and landed both feet onto the broken pavement. There was a moment of silence afterward.

"Bet you won't *dance* on it," came the next dare.

The thing is, I loved dancing. I watched *Soul Train* and *American Bandstand* religiously. At home, in my room, I danced for hours in front of a mirror, trying to perfect the moves I'd seen on TV. But I hadn't yet danced in front of people, only my Rottweiler, JoJo.

"There's no music," I told the dare group.

After leaning in and whispering to each other, two girls in the group started singing "Flashlight" by the psychedelic-funk band Parliament. The others joined in with backup vocals, bass lines, and handclaps. My heart raced. I knew every moment of that song. It was one of my favorites to dance to.

I stood on the crack, swaying slowly to the beats they were making. The more I moved, the louder the kids clapped and sang. Pretty soon, I was full-on dancing—a combination of The Hustle, The Bus Stop, and The Funky Chicken, but with some signature leg wiggles, head rolls, and turns that were mine alone.

Other kids came over to watch, adding more claps and sing-alongs.

I heard someone say, "That white boy *can dance.*"

At the end, everyone applauded. Jocelyn beamed at me. For the first time in my life, I felt truly seen.

Suddenly, someone from the dare group informed the audience,

"He danced on a *crack*."

The kids made a collective, "OOOOOOO!"

"Dang, best hope yo' mama don't die," one boy said.

"You done broke your 'ol lady's back, son," an older kid said.

The recess bell rang before I could think of a reply. Trailing behind the other kids, walking toward class, I worried about what I'd done, suddenly noticing every crack in the pavement.

The following week, my Dad, who was a truck driver, got hurt while loading big frozen food boxes into his trailer. At the hospital, he told us how he'd slipped on a patch of ice hidden under a thin blanket of snow and had fallen hard on the cement. If that wasn't bad enough, he said, the heavy boxes had landed on him too. The X-rays showed Dad had a broken back and two cracked ribs.

I told myself that Dad's broken back was just an accident, that it wasn't my fault, but a few days into his hospital stay, another bad thing happened. It was Saturday morning. I was in the living room watching *Soul Train* when I heard Mom on the phone.

"Oh my *god*, yes, that's our dog!" She cried.

I guess JoJo had gotten out the back door when no one was looking. We drove three short blocks to Belmont and Ashland and loaded him into the car. Someone said he'd been hit by a bus. The vet told us JoJo's back had been broken, and he would never be able to play, run, or even walk properly again. We had to "let him go," Mom said. She told me it wasn't my fault; I knew otherwise.

With Dad in the hospital and JoJo gone for good, I felt increasingly haunted by what I'd done. I stopped watching dance shows and stopped dancing too. I moved my bed out from under the ceiling crack in my room and stayed away from cracks in the walls as well. But no matter how many cracks I avoided—up, down, or sideways—I couldn't help but accidentally cross some.

At school, it seemed everyone had forgotten about my death-defying crack dance. They pretty much went back to ignoring me, except for Jocelyn, who'd started passing "I like you" notes my way. I returned waves and hellos sheepishly but couldn't bring back the feelings I'd once had for her. It wasn't long before she took her affections elsewhere.

With my heightened awareness of cracks came a fear of looking directly at them, as if seeing one straight-on might make it open and swallow me whole. Afraid to let them go completely, I kept them in my peripheral vision. But in my side view, they shifted and moved around, making them almost more threatening.

One day in homeroom, out of the corner of my eye, I saw a crack in the wall that for sure looked like it was forming letters. Though I tried to stay focused on the blackboard in front of me, I couldn't keep the shape-shifting crack out of my mind. When I finally turned and faced it head-on, the letters were gone, but I had already registered the word they spelled: *closer*.

That night, at home, letters started forming in ceiling cracks above my bed, too. I closed my eyes against them, but the word—the same one as before—had already imprinted itself in my brain.

On the way to school the next day, I saw the word forming in sidewalk cracks as well. I walked in the snow and ice to avoid them, but *closer* popped out of ice cracks, too. Panicking, I ran the rest of the way to school. Luckily, by the time I got there, the word had stopped coming at me. I fell asleep on my desk during first period and was awoken by my homeroom teacher, Mr. Napoli, after the bell rang. He asked if I was ok. I was afraid he knew what I'd done.

Mom and I went to visit Dad in the hospital that night. After we'd been there a few minutes, I said I had to go to the bathroom. It was just too depressing seeing Dad like that. Roaming the hallways, I got turned around and walked into a janitor's closet by accident. I would've backed out right away, but I saw something on the wall that stopped me. In flowing cursive writing, as if written by the hand of Jocelyn Ramirez, *closer* was throbbing in a plaster crack.

Realizing the door had closed behind me, I turned and grabbed the knob. It was locked. I pounded and yelled, but no one came. After a few minutes, realizing there was no choice, I faced the crack. Just as I had obeyed Jocelyn that fateful morning at recess, I had to obey the word popping through the plaster.

"What do you *want*?" I yelled at the crack.

There was total silence. More than silence, it was like all the sound had been sucked out of the little room. I'm not sure how to describe what happened next. It was like hearing, but the sounds came from inside rather than out. And then other sense experiences—sights, smells, feelings—emerged from inside as well, showing me glimpses of the past—snippets of the most painful times in my life—as if they were happening right then in the present moment. The memories, if you could call them that, came and went, taking over my body, rattling me. One of them showed my mother leaving me at a grocery store when I was three. Another showed the time I fractured my arm jumping into a pool when I was six. Strangely, things about my parents and their pasts started coming through as well. Mom, as a lonely little girl, receiving almost no care or attention from her own parents. Dad, as a young man, downhearted as he made the decision to quit college when Mom got pregnant. Then I saw Mr. Napoli struggling with the death of a loved one. And it didn't stop there. The painful visions just kept coming and coming. I witnessed horrible events happening to kids I knew from class—Steve finding his junkie dad overdosed, Carlos's family being deported back to Mexico. There were even people—kids and grownups—that I didn't recognize, every one of them going through something terrible. It was all too much. I collapsed against the wall and started crying.

And that's when I fell through the crack.

I wasn't in a closet anymore. I wasn't even in the world anymore. There was no pain or suffering there, mine or anyone else's. There was only vast, endlessly dark space. It was beautiful.

Before I had a chance to think about what was happening, I felt someone's hand on my shoulder.

"Oh my God, Ryan! We were so worried about you," Mom yelled from behind the janitor—the exact words she'd used after the grocery store incident.

When we got home, I heard Mom on the phone whispering to someone. The only thing I could make out was,

"He was hiding in a closet…I'm sure he knows."

She was wrong, I didn't know. But I found out soon enough.

The next day, when I got home from school, Dad called from the hospital. He told me Mom was leaving him for a guy she met at work and that they were getting a divorce. He asked if I wanted to live with him or her. It was hard to answer. All I could think of was the janitor's closet—the pain and suffering on this side of the crack, and the freedom on the other side. I don't remember what else Dad said, just that he cried a lot.

When we got off the phone, I walked through the apartment inspecting every crack—floors, walls, and ceilings, peripherally and straight—but I didn't see *closer* anywhere. I started moving furniture around, searching for cracks I didn't know about. It took a while, but I finally found one behind a mirror in the bathroom. I set the mirror on the floor and stared at the crack for a long time. Though I didn't fall through, like in the janitor's closet, gazing at the crack calmed me down a bit. And as I became more relaxed, I began to notice things more sharply. First, it was my heart beating and my blood pumping. Then it was the hum of the light and some distant street sounds. As I gave over to the noticings, it seemed like the bathroom was becoming bigger, or like the space itself was growing. Although I wasn't moving, staring at the crack reminded me of dancing—like me and the crack were dance partners and the space and noticings were the music.

I heard Mom turn the key in the front door lock and realized I'd been in the bathroom a long time. She stayed quiet while she cooked dinner and set the table, but as soon as we sat down to eat, she started crying. I felt her sadness inside of me, just like all those experiences in the janitor's closet.

When Dad got out of the hospital, we moved to a new neighborhood about a mile away from the old place. I saw Mom most weekends. Dad got us a new Rottweiler puppy. I named her "Bump"—not after the disco dance like Dad thought, it was just that she bumped into things all the time. I went back to watching *Soul Train* and started dancing again too. But I didn't practice in front of a mirror anymore. I knew I was a good dancer.

That was all a really long time ago. I still see the cracks—not just in solid things like pavement or plaster, but in thoughts and feelings too. They're always showing up, splitting things open, calling me to come closer. When I follow their command, they bring the noticings and the big, fresh space. And the more I let go into that space, the more freely I'm able to dance.

Tonight's Sermon

The people moving swiftly up and down corridors, getting in and out of workstations, talking loudly and slamming doors, cause Gerald's shoulders to squeeze all the way up to his earlobes. At times like this, he imagines the small room where he works to be set squarely in the center of a twelve-sided Rubik's Cube being twisted savagely in the hands of a giant angry child who's never able to line up the colors and solve the puzzle.

"Out there chaos. In here order. Out there chaos…" he repeats, bringing his mind back to the panel of pictures he's meant to decipher.

The door to his little office flings open just then.

"Busy week ahead, Ger-o. You should really get your quota up," Bernie, Gerald's boss, says, slamming the door on his way out.

While the next set of images loads on his monitor, Gerald recalls the sign he saw outside The Vertical Church the night before: *Tonight's Sermon: I Am Not A Robot.*

Below the title were pictures in square panels with a single sentence at the bottom: *Select all images that look like Jesus.*

Of the Jesus images on the marquee board, there was one carrying a cross, one hanging on a cross, one with a halo crown, and one with a crown of thorns. Of the non-Jesus images, there was one of war raging, one of a junkie injecting drugs, one of a man stealing an old lady's purse, and one of a woman hitting a child.

Given his job in the button room, there was no way Gerald could ignore the captcha-inspired signage. He walked into the large brick church, took a seat in a rear pew, and listened attentively.

"We all know what it's like to be told what we should do. People go 'round telling others what they *should* do all day long," the pastor began, inspiring a few chuckles. "But when we accept *Jesus* as our Savior we open to *His* truth. For *Jesus* unlocks that within us that which *knows* what is right and what is wrong, which one is *God's* command, and which one is Satan's *temptation*. Brothers 'n sisters, we have a *moral* captcha to maneuver in every situation and with every person. Not on a computer screen, but in our God-given, ever-lovin' hearts. Say it with me now... I am *not* a robot!"

"I am *not* a robot!" Gerald says, poking the big red button on his computer's keypad, correctly signing off on a captcha with a full thirty seconds to spare. Then, as he does every time he answers a challenge correctly, Gerald picks up the six-sided Rubik's Cube on his desk and gives it one quick twist.

Reaching into his jacket, Gerald fishes out a pocket-sized religious tract given to him after the church service. The three-word title—*Are You Ready?*—along with a black-and-white drawing of an industrial clock on the document's cover, immediately reactivates Gerald's shoulder/earlobe tension. Seesawing between curiosity and aversion—shoulders down, shoulders up—Gerald finally flips the pamphlet open to the second page where he finds a sketch of a nuclear mushroom cloud exploding outside the window of a home. Inside the home, a couple and their children are filling a "go bag" with a numbered list of items: *1. Bible 2. Prayer 3. God's love 4. Food 5. Flashlight 6. Raincoat*

Gerald stares out the tiny window of his tiny office, imagining the puffy clouds in the distance to be the product of a nuclear bomb. An alert on his computer rings just then, reminding him that his time to answer the next captcha has expired. Gerald returns his attention to the screen as a new set of pictures loads. He gets back to clicking images, blazing through the rest of the day with his focus intact. Trees. Rubik twist. Fire trucks. Rubik twist. Airplanes. Rubik twist. Ladders. Rubik twist…

At the end of the day, Gerald takes the crowded elevator twenty-three stories down to street level and steps into the brisk evening, being watchful, as the Pastor warned, of the moral captchas he is bound to encounter.

Several events on the walk home perk Gerald's curiosity:

A man bumping into him on the sidewalk without apologizing.

A couple kissing in public.

Litter being thrown from a passing car.

A teenager in a doorway holding a cardboard sign that reads: *Anything Helps.*

Uncertain which are God's commands and which are Satan's temptations, Gerald takes his best guess in each situation, imaginarily pressing the big red button and tangibly twisting his Rubik's Cube at the completion of each moral captcha.

When he arrives home, Gerald retrieves a backpack from the closet—the one his mother gave him for his twenty-ninth birthday—and starts prepping a go bag. He stuffs a flashlight, canned tuna, a windbreaker, and an extra Rubik's Cube inside, but because he doesn't own a Bible, and is unsure how to place "prayer" or "God's love" into a bag, Gerald determines it would be best to speak with the Pastor before continuing.

The next morning, Gerald straps on his half-full go bag and stops at the Vertical Church on the way to work. Finding the front door unlocked, he roams the empty chapel and halls until he hears voices emanating from an office.

"Excuse me, reverend sir. My name's Gerald. I saw your sermon two nights ago…"

"Got another one, Sally!" The Pastor calls over his shoulder.

"You've come to the right place!" Sally says, entering the room cheerily.

"Are you ready to accept Jesus as your personal Lord and Savior, Jerry?" The Pastor asks.

"It's Gerald, sir," Gerald answers.

"Will you follow His command from this day forth?"

Gerald nods his head weakly while readying his lips to ask a question. Before he can utter a word, the Pastor and Sally close their eyes tightly and begin praying.

"Heavenly Father, we bring you this lost and weary soul who comes seeking your salvation…"

Gerald, having deduced that keeping Satan's temptation out of one's field of vision is a necessary precursor to letting Jesus in, squeezes his eyelids shut too. *Out there chaos. In here order*, he tells himself.

When the church people get to the "amen" part, Gerald peeks his left eye open enough to see Sally filling a Dixie cup at the office sink.

"In the name of the Father, the Son, and the Holy Spirit, I baptize thee!" The Pastor effuses, flicking tap water at the bald spot on back of Gerald's head.

How do you feel *now*, son?" The Pastor asks.

"Good, I guess. Real good."

"Hear that, Sal? This fella's feeling real *good*! That's *Jesus* in your heart. He'll be *walking* and *talking* with you now, Harold."

"Gerald, sir. The thing is, I'm in need of some items… for my go bag."

Promising to return for Sunday service to learn more about God's love, Gerald purchases a Bible for nineteen dollars—"at cost" the reverend says—and hurries off to work.

Outside, as Gerald finishes tucking the good book into his backpack, he suddenly sees it…

A yellow car drives through a yellow light nearly running over a pedestrian wearing a yellow jacket. Gerald takes down the license, vowing to call the police when he gets to work.

A block later, he spots a red bird flying over a sunburnt man who's panhandling next to a fire hydrant. Gerald drops a few coins into the man's cup and wishes him good luck.

Then, as he nears the office, Gerald sees a woman drop a green scarf on the green grass near a green trash can. He quickly fetches it from the ground and returns it to her.

God's command is just like Rubik's Cube! He thinks.

When he arrives at his little office in the giant building, Gerald pushes his go bag under the desk, takes his seat confidently, and flips on the computer. Still elated from his moral captcha breakthrough, it takes a moment to register the peculiar images materializing on his monitor. The usual nine square panels appear—three down, three across—but what's inside them makes Gerald's face scrunch. Confusedly, he clicks the refresh icon—something he rarely does—and shakes his head as the next captcha loads. Not only can Gerald not understand what he's looking at, there are no written prompts indicating what objects he should be looking for. On top of that, the computer's color contrast seems to have gone out. Clicking the refresh tab a second time, Gerald scours the new captcha for clues but can't find any similarities between the nine black-and-white, blob-like images occupying his screen.

An alarm goes off above Gerald's computer letting him know his time has run out. Bernie flings the door open just then.

"We've moved up to level four, Ger-o. They're more difficult now. You'll have to maintain your quota to stay on the team."

Three hours later, after a bitter morning of misidentifying captchas, Gerald decides to take an early lunch outside. Before he gets to the elevator, Bernie waves him into the big office. Gerald nods along with the lips flapping, the words coming toward him, but nothing Bernie is saying lands.

On a bench in a nearby park, Gerald opens his go bag and pulls out a ham and cheese sandwich. As he nibbles distractedly, a sudden realization pushes all other thoughts aside:

No one has ever explained what the captchas are for.

While his shoulders and earlobes reach toward one other with an excruciating level of tension, Gerald seeks out rationalizations for the troubling predicament he's in.

It was enough to find a job I was good at, it was enough that no one bothered me at work, it was enough that Mother was happy having me out of the house… it's not my fault no one told me!

But right now, sensing that the button room may well be Satan's temptation and not God's command, none of those thoughts are enough to lift the burden of responsibility from his painfully compressed shoulders.

Finishing his last bite of sandwich, Gerald pulls his Rubik's Cube from the backpack and gives it one hard twist.

Bernie has some explaining to do, he thinks.

Gathering his lunch garbage, Gerald stands and marches toward the solitary trashcan at the park's exit. But the overfull bin, he soon discovers, leaves no room for his rubbish. As he angrily stuffs the wrappers into his own pants' pocket, a woman's scream suddenly cuts through the air.

"Help! He has my purse!"

Ransacking the purloined purse, the thief—a scraggly man in a hoodie about Gerald's height and build—runs toward the exit and, consequently, toward Gerald. In the blink of an eye, Gerald palms his Rubik's Cube, winds up, and hurls it at the robber's head. The brightly colored puzzle rotates through space, hits the purse-snatcher's forehead, and crashes on the pavement. A moment later, as if in slow motion, Gerald watches as the thief's fist closes in on his face.

"How you feeling sweetie? When you didn't come home, I called your office. The secretary told me they let you go today. Is that why you were fighting in the park?"

As he scrutinizes his mother, Gerald wonders if she's sick or simply isn't wearing makeup. Before he can give the matter another thought, a large picture is shoved in front of him.

"No concussion. Just a nasty contusion around your left eye. Probably want to ice it a little more when you get home," the doctor says, pointing at the X-ray.

Gerald squints at the black-and-white image then lifts his gaze to the black-and-white industrial clock hanging over the door. Reaching down for his shoes, he realizes they're black-and-white as well. Shockingly, it dawns on Gerald that the entire room and its contents—the medical items, the bed, the landscape print on the wall, the nurse, the doctor, and his mother—are all black, white, or some combination of the two.

"Where's my *Rubik's Cube*?!?" Gerald blurts out.

"Oh, yes. Apparently, a woman gave it to the ambulance driver when they came for you. It's just there, next to the bed," the nurse points.

Gerald investigates the six-sided puzzle, now missing a corner from its earlier collision. He rotates the cube this way and that, but no matter which way he arranges the rows, they remain solid gray—no colors to line up, no puzzle to solve.

In the car, while his mother chats nervously, Gerald gazes silently out the passenger window. Three blocks from their house, as they near the Vertical Church, he suddenly exclaims,

"Let me out here."

"I will do no such thing. You've had a serious injury, hon."

"Stop the car *now!*"

When his mother stops at the next light, Gerald leaps from the car and dashes down the street.

Bursting into the church, he finds a custodian sweeping aisles.

"Where is he?" Gerald asks.

"Who you looking for?"

"The Pastor."

"Ain't no church Tuesday night. He be here tomorrow."

"Is this… are we in level four?"

"If this level… *what?*"

"The *moral captcha*. Is this level four?!?"

As Gerald continues yelling, the janitor unscrews the long handle from the broom's head and holds it up like a bat.

"Best leave on yo' own feet 'fore I go upside yo' head."

Heeding the warning, Gerald leaves the building hastily, passing the marquee board out front that bears a new black-and-white message: *Tonight's Sermon: Eternal Happiness or Eternal Heat—Your Choice*

Up and down streets and boulevards, through alleys and parking lots, Gerald runs until his sides ache. Eventually he slows to a fast walk and then to a slower one. Sometime later, in a part of town unfamiliar to him, Gerald takes a seat on a curb. A broken bottle in the gutter catches a glint of light from a streetlamp overhead. Gerald picks up the biggest chunk and runs its jagged edge against his tender skin again and again, feeling chaos and order blend, black into white, until his tired gray eyes droop and finally close.

Pierce

"He just won't listen, James!"

"Did you go through the steps like we talked about?"

"You don't know what it's like when you're gone for *weeks* at a time."

"You knew what I did for a living when we met."

"I thought you might consider your son's welfare at some point…"

"Nope. Don't want to go there, Lis. My job supports this family."

"I'm just so… I'm frustrated, *James!*"

"Oh, for Christsake. Let me unpack my gear then I'll talk to him."

After locking his gun in a cabinet and emptying his suitcase, James gives a listen at Joshua's door. The inharmonious sounds emanating from within—a mixture of electronic whirring and buzzing and heavy metal grunting and grinding—make him grimace.

"Josh… it's Dad."

From down the hall, Lisa shoots her "just do it" look. James tightens his already tight jaw, twists the knob of his thirteen-year-old's door, and pushes through the barricade of dirty clothes, food scraps, and computer equipment.

When Joshua won't look up from the computer, James places his hand on the boy's shoulder.

The scream that comes out of his son just then is horrific enough, James thinks, to make his neighbors wonder if someone is being tortured right there in the Pierce home. Removing the unwanted hand, James retreats to the hall where Lisa is looming with folded arms and her "I told you so" look.

James closes the door, shaking his head.

"It's bad," he says.

"It's *really* bad," Lisa confirms.

In the kitchen, the couple aim weary eyes at one another until Lisa starts crying.

"Time for level five," James says coolly.

"You and your goddamn levels. This is not *Gitmo*, James!"

With renewed firmness, James pushes open his son's door, makes his way to the computer, and yanks each of the overfull power strips from the wall with a meaningful grunt.

"What's the matter with you?!?" Joshua yells.

"I'm your *father* and I have a duty to you, to your mother, and to our country to deal with your behavior. You've given me no choice. It's not just your computer this time. I'm taking away your name."

"You can't take…wait. What?"

"You heard me. You're not Joshua anymore. From now on you're just 'hey you' or 'hey kid.' Understand?"

James watches confusion turn to panic on his son's face and then lifts the computer monitor, marching out the door with cords and video game accessories dragging behind him.

"*Thompson, Renee.*"

"Here."

"Simmons, Edward."

"Here."

"Pierce, Joshua."

When no response comes, Mr. Lutkus, the kid's aged homeroom teacher, lowers his readers, peers out at the room, and calls again.

"Joshua Pierce, are you *present?*"

The kid raises his hand sheepishly.

"Why don't you speak up, son?" Mr. Lutkus asks.

"I have a note," the kid says.

The teacher waves the boy to the front of the room and takes the neatly folded letter from his hand. As he finishes reading the two-sentence message typed below an official government letterhead, Mr. Lutkus raises his thick gray eyebrows and takes a deep breath.

"I see," he says. "Well, have a seat... *you.*"

At recess, a few kids from class read the note left on the teacher's desk. Word soon spreads of the boy who no longer has a name.

At eighteen, when the kid graduates high school, he enlists in the Army to get as far away from home as possible and to shoot real guns instead of electronic ones. The military-issue shirts he receives at basic training have his last name, Pierce, emblazoned over the right breast pocket. It's heartening for him to be among young men, like himself, who are known by last names only.

After two years of active duty overseas, Pierce returns to the States and takes a job as an electrician—a trade he learned in the military—where he once again keeps the company of men who respond to last names only.

At twenty-one, Pierce marries Sophia, the sister of his Army buddy "Schlotsky," at St. Edward the Confessor church in her hometown of Appleton, Wisconsin. As the priest finishes the ceremony he says,

"I now pronounce you Mister and Missus Pierce."

Pierce cringes at the word "Mister" as it sounds too much like a first name.

"Pierce and Missus Pierce," Pierce corrects.

The priest, taken aback, glances into the groom's eyes and quickly amends his wedding pronouncement.

Three months after he turns twenty-three, Pierce's wife becomes pregnant. When the ultrasound informs the couple that their baby is a boy, Sophia excitedly begins talking names.

"A Bible name. Don't you think he needs a Bible name?" She asks, though it's clearly more of a statement.

The half-smile on Pierce's face indicates his lack of interest in, but amenability to, her decision.

Over the next several days, as Sophia goes through her list of Bible names, she begins repeating one more than the others. As the selection gains momentum in her mind, she starts humming and then singing a popular hymn based on the chosen Bible character.

"Joshua fought the battle of Jericho. Jericho. Jericho. Joshua fought the battle of Jericho and the walls come tumbling down..."

Pierce, no longer offering his usual half-smile, objects firmly to the name. Sophia is crestfallen—not only by the rejection, but by the hardness in her husband she had hoped would soften with parenthood.

By the time Isaiah is born, Pierce is spending the majority of his hours on the job or at a bar among last-name-only men. Sophia shifts the entirety of her love and attention to their child.

A rare phone call from Pierce's mother comes one evening while he's working a twelve-hour at a nearby power plant. When he arrives home late that night, Pierce finds the dinner leftovers waiting on the kitchen table along with a note written in the utilitarian style he and Sophia have come to employ with one other:

George Washington Univ. Hospital. He's dying.

After a sleepless night, Pierce calls in sick for the first time in his life, and books a flight to D.C. He doesn't bother packing the suitcase Sophia left next to the couch for his travel.

As the plane makes its descent toward Ronald Reagan Airport, the pilot informs the passengers of the local time and weather.

"Local time and weather," Pierce repeats, viewing the Washington Monument through the porthole window, like a finger pointing up at him.

Arriving at the hospital, Pierce is led through the cancer ward by a young nurse. They stop, finally, at a door with *Pierce, James* written in purple marker on a wipe board.

"Who are you?" His father asks.

"Pierce."

"That's my name."

"It's your *son*, Mr. Pierce," the thoughtful nurse says.

"Oh. How are you, kid?"

"I want my name back."

"What?"

"You heard me."

"I don't make those decisions anymore," James says resignedly.

Holding his father's gaze a few moments, Pierce leans over the bed and whispers something in the old man's ear. He watches confusion turn to panic on his father's face before stepping out of the room.

As the door closes behind him, Pierce pulls a carefully folded handkerchief from his pocket and rubs his father's name—first and last—off the wipe board.

When he returns home, Pierce greets his wife with the half-smile she hasn't seen since before their son was born. Isaiah, as if expressing the welling emotions in his mother, or the buried ones in his father, cries uncontrollably in Sophia's arms.

The Microphone

"Anyone see us?"
"No one even knew about it."
"How're you so sure?"
"It was on a broken lectern with junk lying all around it."

Sam knew microphones. No doubt about it. But he didn't know a thing about stealing. I, on the other hand, had been in and out of custody so many times I still woke up in the middle of the night thinking the toilet would be next to my bed.

The microphone in question—an "Electro-Voice 664 high fidelity cardioid dynamic," as Sam was always saying—was an old vocal mic with a streamlined 1950s space-age design. They weren't usually worth much, according to Sam, but the one we nabbed was special. It had a slightly different shape. An extra notch in the middle where the engineer's initials—"LB" for Lou Burroughs—had been etched. It was a prototype, Sam said. One of its kind. That alone wasn't enough to make it real valuable, but Sam knew something else about it, too. Namely, that it had been used by Hank Williams Sr.

The only "proof" I saw before agreeing to look for the thing was a grainy black-and-white photo Sam showed me of Hank at the Skyline Club in Austin just before he died. The mic in the picture looked similar enough and, like I said, Sam knew his stuff when it came to microphones. I guess what convinced me, though, was finding out the Electro-Voice 664 didn't hit the market 'til 1954. The picture of Hank was from December '52.

"The problem will be finding the right buyer."

He got that part right. I knew fences, but no one I'd trust with that piece.

We drove to my place in Bucktown since I lived closest to the college. Of course, I knew better than to risk my job—not to mention the possibility of a parole violation—but Sam said the thing was worth fifty grand, minimum. I guess I believed him. At least I wanted to.

When we got to my apartment I put on a pot of coffee. I like the dark stuff. Bustelo. Got the habit from a Puerto Rican chick I dated in Humboldt Park the last time I was out. Sam kept looking out the window, like he suspected someone followed us. I closed the blinds and laid the mic on the desk I use for a table. Sam sat down and stared at the thing like it was a crystal ball. I drank my mud, mulling over how I'd come to know this crazy fucker in the first place...

I'd been pushing broom at the school for about three months when he came on crew. I ignored him in the beginning. He didn't ignore me. I'm not sure how many people at the college knew I was an ex-con. My jailhouse sleeves poked out a bit at the cuffs and my neck tattoo probably saw light of day when I bent over, but I didn't think the average Joe would notice or care about a janitor's tats. Sam went right at it.

"You get those inside?" He asked his first week there.

I asked what he knew about it. He said he'd known people who'd done time, that's all.

You'd never guess Sam was into H by looking at him. I mean to say, the guy was all right angles. Square as they come. At least on the outside. When he offered me a taste one day,

I was kind of surprised but not interested. My tangle with hard stuff had ended years before that.

Sam got high at lunchtime most Fridays. He'd come out of the john half on the nod talking about sound equipment. It was boring, but less boring than eating lunch alone. Other than giving him a lift home now and again, that's all there was to our "friendship." Then one day he brought in a photo of an Electro-Voice, saying that once-upon-a-time they were used in schools like ours. He asked if I'd keep an eye out for something like that, since I cleaned the whole fine arts department, including the auditorium. I didn't bite. A few weeks later, he brought in the picture of Hank, and said he had "reason to believe" that special mic, the prototype, was in the school somewhere…

While I paced my apartment, thinking about our next move, Sam pulled out his gear and started cooking a bag at my desk, without even asking. That pissed me off. As I was about to say something he blurted out,

"Ernie, you're the only one I can tell this to…"

He found a vein, registered, and slammed his dope real fast like a pro. I watched his pupils turn to pinholes and then noticed all the tracks on his arm. The guy was more than the weekend warrior I'd made him out to be.

"Not just Hank…"

His eyelids folded.

"There were others."

He was getting pale.

"Their souls, Ernie…"

His lips turned blue around the edges. I got scared and slapped his face. He opened his eyes just then.

"Their souls are trapped inside…"

"Sam!" I yelled as he slumped forward.

When a guy ODs in your apartment and you're on parole with a stolen microphone lying on the desk you use for a table I guess you don't call 911. I didn't anyway. But even if I had, it would've been too late.

I paced my apartment drinking Bustelo and cursing Sam. I could see myself back in the joint shitting next to my bed again. I tried to make sense of what he'd said, wondering if he was totally off his rocker or what.

My first problem was getting Sam's body out of my place. I didn't want it coming back on me. As I got his gear together, I noticed the glassine baggie the dope came in. There was a brand name stamped on it like the stuff they sell in NYC. It said "Fireball." I smelled it. It was strong to the nose.

When it got dark out, I zipped Sam into a sleeping bag. I waited until the whole building was asleep before pulling my van around back. He wasn't a big guy, but damn he was heavy. The best thing I could figure was to drop him on the Westside near a major drug zone.

I drove 'til I found an empty alley, hauled him out, and dropped him on the ground. The zipper was stuck on the sleeping bag. I kept yanking at it, which only made it worse. As I was wrestling the bag off him, an envelope fell out of his clothes. That fucked with my head. It hadn't occurred to me to check his pockets. I stuck the envelope down my pants, leaned Sam against an abandoned building, and got the hell out of there.

When I was back at my place I emptied the envelope onto the table. It was full of photos but not as grainy as the one of Hank. They were promo pictures. Headshots. I recognized the people. Billie Holiday. Janis Joplin. Jim Morrison. Each of them was singing into an Electro-Voice 664. When I looked real close, I could see the little notch with the initials etched into it. It was the same mic lying on my desk at that very moment.

On Monday, I was back to sweeping floors and plunging toilets. No one seemed to notice about Sam, or the microphone for that matter. Even so, I worried people were looking at me funny.

Two days later, the boss called us in at lunchtime saying he'd gotten word from the authorities that Sam had overdosed. There was no mention of a memorial or anything. The cops never came around, or if they did, I didn't see them. I didn't know what to do with the mic, but I didn't want it at my place. The only thing I could think was to take it back to the college and stash it in a bathroom air vent while I figured my next move.

A couple weeks after that, and still no heat on the Sam situation, I went by his apartment in Bridgeport. There was an open transom window over the back door. I wasn't so slim anymore, but I made it through. The first thing I noticed were the bare white walls. It was completely undecorated. No pictures. No plants. Nothing personalized at all. The only furniture was a table, two chairs, a bed, and a dresser. I went through the drawers—socks, underwear, t-shirts, not much. But underneath the dresser, I found another envelope with pictures inside. In one of the shots was a medieval-looking, wavy blade knife enclosed in a glass case. It had the same insignia, the "LB", that was etched on the mic. Another photo showed a closeup of an old leather-bound book titled *Libertas Bestiae*. I understood then that the letters on the Electro-Voice weren't Lou Burroughs's initials after all. I also understood that if Sam was crazy, he was part of a *bigger* crazy, and I wanted nothing to do with it.

I tried to put it all out of my head. I even considered quitting my job, but the terms of my parole required gainful employment and I didn't have any other prospects. I stuck it out.

Whenever I scrubbed the john where the mic was stashed, I thought about Sam. I also thought about fifty thousand bucks and how I'd spend it. One day, when I was in there cleaning the mirror, I locked the door behind me and pulled the Electro-Voice out of the vent. It felt heavier than I remembered. For some reason, right then, I looked in the mirror and held the mic up to my mouth. I was just goofing off, because, believe me, I'm no singer. But all of a sudden, a beautiful melody came out of me. It was effortless. I could see my lips moving and hear myself singing, but it wasn't at all my voice. A knock came just then.

"Yeah, be right out," I said.

I flushed the toilet and put the mic back quick. When I opened the door, the director of the theatre department was standing on the other side.

"Oh... hi. Thought you were one of our performers when I heard you in there."

I had to think fast.

"Me? No. Never. It was just the radio."

"Really? It sounded so *live*, so rich. What's the name of that song?"

"Oh, man. I don't know. I was just flipping the dial."

I got out of there before he could dig any deeper. Shuffling past the young singers and actors doing warmups in the auditorium, I rolled my mop bucket out to the hall and kept my head down 'til the shift was over.

When I walked out of work that evening, two big guys came out of nowhere and hustled me into a black sedan. I figured them for undercovers. I was sure it had to do with Sam. One pushed me in the back and climbed in next to me, the other got behind the wheel and started driving. In the passenger seat was a well-dressed old man wearing purple glasses. He was no cop.

The old guy leaned over and asked plainly, "Where is it?"

When I didn't answer, the big dude on my right punched me in the side of the head. Hard.

"Where is it, Ernie?"

Hearing my name like that, I thought I was gonna puke. I knew I was about to get thumped again too. Just then a strange idea flashed in my mind.

"*Libertas Bestiae!*"

I don't know if I said it right, but when those words came out of me, they were loud and musical, like something from an opera. It was the same voice from the mirror, only more powerful. The old man looked shocked, almost pained when he heard it. The guy next to me looked stunned too. I took advantage of the confusion and jumped out of the car, doing a barrel roll into oncoming traffic. Cars slammed on brakes in both directions. I was on my feet and deep into the neighborhood before they could get to me.

I hid in a gangway 'til sundown, knowing it wasn't safe to go home or back to work. When I finally got up the nerve, I ran to the El and caught a northbound train to Uptown. I spent my last few bucks on a chicken wire room at The Wilson Men's Hotel. The place was full of vagrants, winos, and day laborers. Seemed as good a place as any to hide.

The next day, with no money and no other options, I went back to my old ways—breaking and entering. I had always been a good burglar. In and out. No muss, no fuss. I could tell by a person's furnishings where their valuables were likely to be hid. My specialty, though, was lifting tchotchkes. "Tacky treasures," as my ma used to call them. I knew which ones were worth something, and those little goodies were usually hiding in plain sight.

The other thing I took up again was shooting dope. I went from zero to dopefiend in a week. I guess the shit on the street had gotten stronger since the days when I was chipping. Pretty soon, I didn't care if I had a roof over my head or not. I slept on loading docks, alleys—anyplace I could score a bag in a hurry when I woke up.

Stealing and slamming wasn't what I planned to be doing at thirty-five years old. But what I really hadn't counted on was the singing. It wasn't the same as the day I did it in the mirror—not as powerful—but I could still carry a tune better than most. They were made-up songs, I guess. At least I didn't recognize them when they came out of me. The weirdest part, though, is that I wasn't even trying to sing. I didn't even want to do it. But I had to. It was like I needed to get something out of my system, something I needed other people to hear before I could let it go. The thing is, no matter how many songs I sang, more kept coming. Guys on the street started calling me "Smackhead Sinatra." It stuck.

The heavier my habit got, the bolder the burglaries became, and the lazier I was about where I did them. Pretty soon, I was pulling jobs in the middle of the day up and down the same blocks I'd already hit. One day, coming out a window with my pillowcase full of knick-knacks, I got nabbed. I was almost relieved to see the men in blue waiting on the sidewalk. Maybe I had been trying to get caught. When they slapped the cuffs on me, I started singing.

"Looks like *Smackhead Sinatra* is our Bric-a-Brac Bandito," one of the coppers said.

I didn't know my moniker had made it all the way to the precinct.

I was given the max, seven years, for the breaking and entering. They tacked on another five for the parole violation. I copped a plea so I wouldn't have to sit in Cook County Jail waiting for trial. That gladiator school is no place for an old con.

Soon enough, I was back in the pen with a toilet next to my bed, which, incidentally, comes in handy when you're kicking dope. It's not that I couldn't get drugs inside, I had just lost the appetite once I was back in the big house. Funny thing, you can get heroin in prison but not Bustelo. I would've paid plenty for that dark roast. I made do with the generic instant they sold at commissary.

As soon as the junk was out of my system the singing stopped too. I couldn't've made a melody if I tried. No more smackhead, no more Sinatra. Just plain old Ernie Bardo. Inmate number A17589.

I got back into the routine soon enough. Keeping my head down. Killing time. Shooting the breeze with a couple guys I knew from previous incarcerations. I never talked about the mic. Not that any of those clowns would've believed me anyway.

About six months into my stretch, I was watching the tube and saw a clip on the local news. It was a hometown-girl-makes-good kind of thing. I recognized her right away. She was one of the pretty students from the college's theatre department. The anchorman said she'd just won big on a music competition show, scoring a contract with a major label. They showed her rocking out hard for the judges, and, yeah, she was singing into that Electro-Voice 664.

Anyone could tell by her moves and voice that she was a star in the making. Those of us savvy to a junkie's ways could see she was on stuff—the deep circles under the eye makeup gave that away. But I was probably the only one watching that night who saw the total desperation in the girl's face.

Of course, Shawna Taylor became a household name overnight. Seemed like everybody knew the words to her damn songs that fast too. There was nowhere, I mean *nowhere*, you could go in the prison to get away from them. It got so bad I finally stabbed a guy one cell over when he wouldn't shut up with that noise. Truth is, I wanted to go to the hole so I wouldn't have to hear them anymore.

When they put me in isolation it felt like I could finally breathe again. I cleaned the toilet and tucked in the sheets, setting up my new space to get comfy for the long stretch ahead. But that night, when the guard was making his rounds, I heard whistling. And yeah, it was one of her songs. I tried stuffing my ears with toilet paper, covering my head with a pillow, yelling over the sound, but everything I did seemed to amplify it instead of drown it out…

It's gotten to the point now where day and night, guard or no guard, the songs just keep coming. They call this solitary confinement, but I have so many cellmates. Hank, Billie, Jim, Janis. Shawna. There are others too. People whose names I don't know. Each one of them trying to out-sing the rest. Each one trying, impossibly, to sing their way out of here.

Acknowledgments

Many thanks to the magazines who first published these stories:

"Your Place in This World" - *Third Wednesday Magazine*
"Liberty Bell" - *The Razor*
"Pick a Part" - *The Museum of Americana*
"Triple Feature" - *Bear Paw Arts Journal*
"March 15th" - *The MacGuffin*
"Sponsors" - *Exacting Clam*
"Self-help" - *Berlin Literary Review*
"Mall Doors - *NUNUM*
"Mashed Potato Time" - *The Inquisitive Eater*
"Closer" - *The Hooghly Review*
"Tonight's Sermon" - *Progenitor Literary Journal*
"Pierce" - *Fiction on the Web*
"The Microphone" - *Revolution John Journal*

* * *

My deep thanks also to the early readers, advice-givers, and supporters who helped me along the way: Annika

Gunderson, Louis Greenstein, Traven La Botz, Dan La Botz, and Jonah Goger.

Last, I'd like to thank the Cornerstone Press team, especially publisher Dr. Ross Tangedal, who took a chance on this cold-calling, newbie writer and the clumsy, unedited batch of stories he sent to Cornerstone.

JAKE LA BOTZ is a touring musician, actor, and fiction writer whose work has appeared in *Third Wednesday, Mojo Journal, The Razor, Exacting Clam*, and several other venues. He has been shortlisted for the J.F. Powers Prize and nominated for the Pushcart Prize. He lives in St. Paul, Minnesota, with his wife and youngest daughter.

www.ingramcontent.com/pod-product-compliance
Lightning Source LLC
LaVergne TN
LVHW040053080526
838202LV00045B/3608